TURBULENCE

DAVID SZALAY

SCRIBNER

New York   London   Toronto   Sydney   New Delhi

SCRIBNER
An Imprint of Simon & Schuster, Inc.
1230 Avenue of the Americas
New York, NY 10020

Copyright © 2018 by David Szalay

Originally published in Great Britain in 2018 by Jonathan Cape, an imprint of Vintage Publishing, a division of Penguin Random House UK.

First Scribner hardcover edition July 2019

SCRIBNER and design are registered trademarks of The Gale Group, Inc., used under license by Simon & Schuster, Inc., the publisher of this work.

For information about special discounts for bulk purchases, please contact Simon & Schuster Special Sales at 1-866-506-1949 or business@simonandschuster.com.

The Simon & Schuster Speakers Bureau can bring authors to your live event. For more information or to book an event, contact the Simon & Schuster Speakers Bureau at 1-866-248-3049 or visit our website at www.simonspeakers.com.

Interior design by Erich Hobbing

Manufactured in the United States of America

1   3   5   7   9   10   8   6   4   2

Library of Congress Cataloging-in-Publication Data is available.

ISBN 978-1-9821-2273-7
ISBN 978-1-9821-2275-1 (ebook)

For T & B

TURBULENCE

1

LGW–MAD

On the way home from the hospital, she asked him if he wanted her to stay. "No, I'll be fine," he said.

She asked him again later that afternoon. "I'll be *fine*," he said. "You should go home. I'll look at flights."

"Are you sure, Jamie?"

"Yes, I'm sure. I'll look at flights," he said again, and he already had his laptop open.

She stood at the window, unhappily eyeing the street. The view of semidetached Notting Hill villas and leafless little trees was very familiar to her now. She had been there for more than a month, living in her son's flat while he was in the hospital. In January he had been told he had prostate cancer—hence the weeks of radiotherapy in St. Mary's. The doctor had said they would now wait a month and then do some scans to see if the treatment had been successful.

"There's one tomorrow afternoon, at five-ish," he told her. "Iberia. From Gatwick to Barajas. Is that okay?"

She had been privately wondering whether to make the journey by train and ferry. She told herself not to be silly. She knew it was silly, her fear of flying. The statistics spoke for themselves. "Yes," she said. "That's okay."

She turned to face the living room again. Jamie was on the sofa, twisted sideways over the laptop, tapping at it. He had lived in this flat for decades, since his early twenties, all his adult life. There was something neurotic, she thought, about his unwillingness to move. He was in his fifties now, which was strange. She still thought of him as someone young.

"Okay," he said, shutting the laptop, "that's sorted," and she thought how easy it was, these days, to do that—to acquire a plane ticket, to travel around.

He insisted on accompanying her to the airport. They took the Gatwick Express, didn't speak much, and parted when she went through security. She was tearful, which wasn't like her. A minute later, in the snaking security queue, she turned, hoping to find him still there. He wasn't there, and she had the feeling, as if seeing the future, that he was going to die of his illness, that he would be dead within a year. She was still trembling with the force of the sensation as she struggled with the large plastic tub and took off her shoes.

Once she was through security, she went straight into one of the fake pubs in the departure lounge for a Bloody Mary.

She had a second Bloody Mary and then, when her flight was announced, walked to the gate. It turned out to be a significant distance. When she arrived there were a large number of people already queuing there—more, she thought, than the plane would be able to hold. She wondered if they would need volunteers to stay behind. They didn't. She was in a window seat. She looked out at the low sunlight on the gray tarmac. The plane started to move.

Then it stopped.

It seemed to be in some sort of queue itself—in regular sequence, the rumble of jets arrived faintly from somewhere she couldn't see.

The tedium of all this had almost succeeded in sedating her when the pilot's voice, momentarily present in the cabin, muttered, "Prepare for takeoff."

She felt the fear then, even through the vodka, surging up like the sound of the engines in a series of well-defined stages—first one kind of loudness, then another, as she was pressed into her seat and the safe world went past in the window. She never quite believed, at this point in the process, that the plane *would* take off. She always found herself thinking: *Surely it should have happened by now, something must have gone wrong*—and so it always took her by surprise, it was always somehow a profoundly surprising moment when the plane's nose lifted, when the plane pulled itself free of the earth—or the feeling was actually more like the earth was falling away.

Sussex was already quite far down, a bluish patchwork of fields in the dusk.

There was, from somewhere, a quiet ping.

She did not know whether it soothed her or not, that ping. She wondered what it meant. Though it seemed to say that everything was happening normally, it probably meant nothing.

She looked around, as if surprised that she was still alive, and for the first time she noticed the man in the seat next to her.

He was sitting very still with his hands knitted loosely in his lap, staring straight ahead. Perhaps he too was trying to master his fear.

She was going to have to ask him to move at some point.

As soon as the fasten–seat belts sign went off, she turned to him and said, "Excuse me." She pitched her voice nice and loud—it was surprising how loudly you had to speak to be heard over the noise.

Sure enough, the man looked at her in momentary incomprehension, as if he had no idea what she wanted. "Excuse me," she said again.

It was awkward, the way he had to move past the empty aisle seat to let her through. And she wondered, making the same move herself, why he didn't simply *take* the aisle seat, since there was no one there—they would both have more space that way.

When he eventually sat down in the middle seat again, she found herself irritated by his obtuseness. She even wondered whether to suggest to him that he move, and a form of words came to her: *It might be more comfortable for both of us if you sat there?* It was the sort of thing she normally would have said, with an encouraging smile. In this case, however, she worried that the man might infer some sort of prejudice in the suggestion—some sort of racial prejudice—and that was enough on its own to hold her back. She didn't think she was racist but she found it difficult to be sure, which made her self-conscious in situations like this. She wondered whether to speak to the man. He didn't seem to be English. The handful of words he had said to her as they shuffled around each other in the aisle had had what sounded like a French accent.

And anyway, he seemed preoccupied himself, absorbed in his own thoughts, whatever they might be.

With small tinkling noises, like tiny scratches on the underlying roar, a trolley was approaching in the aisle.

She stirred airline Bloody Mary with a little plastic baton. The engines purred in slow rhythmic waves. She felt the vodka work on her. The tightly packed fabric of the world seemed to loosen. Her mind had more primacy over it—her thoughts started to seem like things that were actually happening. Her son's death, for instance, presented itself in a series of images that felt so true they made her silently tearful. She turned to the window and found only her own face in the dark plastic now, deeply shadowed like a landscape at sundown. She imagined herself, after his death, emptying his flat—taking everything down from the shelves, all the stuff that he had held on to so tenaciously for so many years. It was then that the first wobble went through the plane. What she hated about even mild turbulence was the way it ended the illusion of security, the way that it made it impossible to pretend that she was somewhere safe. She managed, thanks to the vodka, more or less to ignore that first wobble. The next was less easy to ignore, and the one after that was violent enough to throw her neighbor's Coke into his lap.

And then the pilot's voice, suddenly there again, and

saying, in a tone of terrifying seriousness, "Cabin crew, take your seats."

In the eerie, provisional stillness when it was over, she opened her eyes and they met those of the man sitting next to her. He was shaken too. Now that the worst of the fear was past he was starting to attend to the spilt Coke on his suit trousers. She handed him some paper tissues and he thanked her, and after that they talked a little, about why they were each on that particular flight. The man told her that he had been in London for work. She asked him what he did. She didn't feel well. The shaken feeling that had followed the fear was turning into something worse, a kind of dizziness. She felt things moving unpleasantly around her and saw in the man's face that she must look terrible. She felt sick. The man was asking her something she wasn't able to make out. He said it several times, and then he stood up and went.

When she opened her eyes again her head seemed to be on the man's seat and she was looking up at a dark-haired woman. The woman was asking her questions in English with a strong Spanish accent. "Are you diabetic?" was one of them, and she managed to nod when she heard it. Then the woman said, "I'm a doctor. I'm here to help you."

"Thank you," she said, not sure if her voice was making any sound, and that was the last thing she was aware of until she was being sick on the floor of the plane. There was a lot of noise and she thought, with her head hanging near the carpet, that the plane must actually be crashing now. Then she understood that it was landing.

They were in an ambulance, she and the Spanish doctor. The paramedics had injected her with something and she felt stronger. She had wanted to go home, and not to the hospital, but apparently that wasn't an option. As the ambulance went sirening through the streets they were sitting inside it, and she was telling the doctor about the turbulence, perhaps forgetting that the woman had been there herself. "I've never been so afraid," she said. "I shut my eyes and told myself to face the fact that I was about to die. I had no doubt that I was about to die. I was sitting there with my eyes shut, and I was thinking: *If I'm going to die, please let Jamie live. Please let him live. Please, please let him live.*" She stopped for a moment, and then said, "I don't normally do things like that. I don't know who I thought I was talking to."

"Maybe it was God?" the doctor suggested with a smile.

"I don't believe in God. That's my point." Aware that she was being oddly open and talkative, and vaguely wondering what it was that the ambulance men had injected her with, she said, "The weird thing is that now I have this hopeful feeling about the whole situation. I was so down about it, and now I have this feeling that it's going to be okay, that Jamie's going to be okay."

The doctor smiled again. The ambulance had stopped. "Here we are," she said.

2

MAD-DSS

Cheikh knew something was wrong when Mohammed wouldn't look him in the eye. "What is it, Mohammed?" he asked him. Mohammed said nothing. He had been waiting at arrivals with some other drivers. The terminal was quiet—it was late, after midnight; the flight from Madrid had been one of the few still to arrive. Mohammed took the suitcase without saying a word. As they stepped into the warm night, Cheikh told him about the turbulence that had hit his flight from London to Madrid, laughing as he described how he had spilled Coca-Cola all over himself, and how he had tried to use a hand dryer in the men's room at Madrid airport to dry his trousers. Mohammed didn't seem to be listening. They stopped at the black Lexus, and he silently stowed the suitcase, and then opened the door for his employer.

"Oh Mohammed," Cheikh said, sprawling in his creased suit across the leather seat. "I am so very tired."

It was always an odd feeling, to start the day in London

or somewhere like that and end it here, in Dakar, at home. The hotel room overlooking the leafless park where he had woken that morning, where he had stood at the window and watched people in dark clothes hurry along the wet asphalt paths, some of them with umbrellas, seemed like something he had dreamed. It was strange to think that the same people would walk along the same paths tomorrow morning, without him being there to see them.

"The Bay of Biscay," he said, trying to find Mohammed's eye in the rearview mirror, "is notorious for turbulence. Did you know that, Mohammed?"

Not meeting his eye, Mohammed just shook his head.

"You didn't know that?"

Cheikh waited for Mohammed to say something.

He didn't.

They had encountered traffic and were moving slowly.

"You didn't know that?" Cheikh said again, and again Mohammed said nothing.

The thing was, Mohammed was usually an encouraging and interested listener. This detached silence was strange.

"What is it, Mohammed?" Cheikh asked.

The man pretended not to hear, and Cheikh wondered whether his wife had threatened to leave him again. Maybe he was embarrassed to talk about it. "Is it Mariama?" Cheikh asked, without delicacy.

"No, sir," Mohammed said.

"What then?"

The traffic moved, and Mohammed, steering around a large pothole, used that as a pretext not to answer.

People walked barefoot by the road. They emerged from the darkness into the dim, shadowy light under one of the streetlamps. Then they disappeared into the darkness again.

As light momentarily fell into the car, Cheikh tugged at the fabric of his trousers, trying to see the extent of the Coke stain.

Yes, that had been what's known as "severe" turbulence. It had lasted for ten minutes or so—it had seemed, in other words, to last forever. Cheikh had been afraid. When it finally ended, in the eerie and provisional stillness that followed, his eyes had met those of the woman sitting next to him. She was English, the woman, and in her seventies probably. Some withdrawn English quality, a way she had of hardly seeming to see him, was all that he had noticed about her until then.

He was dabbing at his lap with a napkin, where the Coke had spilled.

Without saying anything, the woman had offered him some paper tissues from her handbag.

They got talking a bit after that. When he asked her why she was going to Madrid, she said she lived in Spain.

She had been in London visiting her son, she explained. He was not well, she added, folding away her tray table. And he suspected, from the way she said it, with a preoccupied and unhappy look as she folded the table away, that it might be something serious. "I hope it's nothing serious?" he asked.

"Oh, it is quite serious," she said, not shirking the fact.

He was still holding the damp tissues, wondering what to do with them. "I'm sorry to hear that," he said.

When she asked him whether he had children, he tried not to sound too smug about it. "Yes," he said. "I have two sons." He ended up showing her pictures on his phone—she must have asked to see them. He flicked through them, holding the screen where she was able to see it. "This is Amadou," he said, showing her a picture of his elder son, in a Manchester City football shirt, standing astride the moped he loved so much. "And this," he said, swiping past a few other shots, "is Didier. The younger."

Full of pride, unable to stop himself, he told her that Amadou was hoping to go to university in France, and she said, "I'm sure he'll do very well there."

"Inshallah," Cheikh had murmured piously, slipping his phone into the inside pocket of his suit. Then he noticed that the woman didn't seem well. She was suddenly very pale and her eyes looked empty. He asked her if she was okay and she didn't seem to understand him. That was when he went and told one of the flight attendants, who asked over the PA system whether there was a doctor on the flight, which there was, a Spanish woman.

They were in traffic again, the city and its smog thickening around them. Palm trees, their trunks partially whitewashed, lined the road in patchy artificial light.

For the first time he saw Mohammed's eyes in the rearview mirror—they were slightly red as if he'd been in tears.

"What is it, Mohammed?" Cheikh said. "Tell me. Why won't you tell me?"

Mohammed shook his head impatiently.

Cheikh sighed, making a show of his own impatience. He didn't like the way Mohammed kept things from him. "Money?" he asked. "You have a problem with money?"

There was no answer to that.

"If you have a problem with money . . ." Cheikh said, in a tone that suggested he could easily solve such a problem, if Mohammed were only open with him.

"No, sir," Mohammed said.

"Sure?"

"Yes, sir."

The traffic started to move again and Cheikh tiredly massaged his eyes. The hours in Madrid between flights

19

had seemed to last forever. He had looked at ties in Salvatore Ferragamo for a while, wondering whether to buy one out of sheer boredom.

He said to Mohammed, "And you're sure it's not Mariama?"

"No, sir."

"How is Mariama?"

Mohammed just shrugged.

"And the kids?"

Mohammed did not answer this. He seemed in fact to tense up, and Cheikh wondered if something might have happened to one of the children—Mohammed and Mariama had four children. Mariama had been no more than fifteen when the first of them was born—and Cheikh thought how pitifully young that seemed to him now, now that he had a son, Amadou, who was that age, and still so obviously just an innocent kid. Mohammed himself had been older, of course. He was . . . what? Ten years older than her? Something like that. Neither of them exactly literate. There had been problems over the years. Cheikh and his wife had tried to help. There's only so much you can do though. Some things, perhaps, are not meant to be. Some things are meant to be, some things are not meant to be.

Cheikh pressed him. "So they are all well? Your kids."

Mohammed answered with a minimal nod.

"El Hadji," Cheikh said, referring to Mohammed's eldest son—he was almost exactly the same age as Amadou. As small children they had played together, had been friends. Cheikh had permitted that, up to a point. "He's doing well?" he asked.

"Yes, sir," Mohammed said, in a voice that was almost a whisper.

Cheikh was paying for El Hadji's education at a private school. Not the same private school that Amadou went to—the new French lycée in its sleek modern building, with its tennis courts and its Mandarin option—a simpler, more local one. Still, a decent enough school, and El Hadji, though unlikely to go to university in France, would have an opportunity to make something of his life. It pleased Cheikh that he was able to do this, to make such a decisive difference to someone's life, to be a figure of such transformative power in the world of Mohammed's family.

He said, "Then what is troubling you, Mohammed? Do you have something to tell me?"

Yes, Mohammed had something to tell him.

That was suddenly obvious from the way, when Cheikh asked him the question, he just stared straight ahead, with this dead expression in his eyes.

Cheikh found, from nowhere, that he had a quiet hankering for a cigarette. It had been more than a decade since he had quit—Amadou, at five years old, having been told that smoking killed people, had one day asked his father to stop, and Cheikh, after thinking about it for a moment, had stubbed out the cigarette he was in the middle of smoking and promised his son that he would never smoke another. There were not that many people in the world who actually cared about you all that much, and if you were lucky enough to have a few who did, he thought, then surely you owed it to them not to destroy yourself thoughtlessly, surely you owed them some sort of effort. Since that day he had not smoked a single cigarette. He was proud of his will-power. Occasionally, though, at moments of stress, the hankering still came.

"What is it, Mohammed?" he asked in a quieter voice.

They were nearing the house. They were in smaller streets—streets on the hill next to the sea where the smog was thinner and there were larger trees, their stiff dropped leaves littering the asphalt under the streetlights. Outside many of the properties were sentry posts.

They were nearing the house.

There it was, its high metal gates. "Stop," Cheikh said.

Mohammed stopped the car in front of the gates and sat there still staring straight ahead through the windscreen. The headlights lit up part of the white-painted metal of the gates. The paint was speckled with rust.

Here, next to the ocean, with the tall surf chewing away at the foot of the hill, the spread of rust was a never-ending problem.

"You have something to tell me, Mohammed," Cheikh said. "What is it?"

There was a long silence. Then Mohammed said, "Madame will tell you." His hand, as he worked the remote control that opened the gates, was shaking.

Cheikh was afraid. Something terrible, he now understood, was waiting for him inside the house.

With a scraping noise, the gates slid open and they drove in.

"What is it?" Cheikh asked. "Why are there no lights on?"

Mohammed had nothing more to say.

After a few seconds, Cheikh emerged from the car and slowly, as if he was going to his own death, walked up the steps and into the dark house.

3

DSS-GRU

They said the boy was dead. It happened too quickly for Werner to follow. There was a sudden smash and the taxi squealed to a stop, making him lean sharply into his seat belt. Nothing too serious seemed to have happened. The taxi driver said some swearwords in French as he pulled on the hand brake. He would obviously have to get out—there would be words to be had. Werner assumed it wouldn't take long. At first he didn't move from his seat in the back of the taxi, an ancient Mercedes, probably an early 1980s model, and the color of swimming-pool tiles. Most of the taxis in Dakar were like that.

He sat there waiting for the driver to do what he needed to do, so that they could be on the move again. He was thinking about Sabine, the woman in Frankfurt he was sort of seeing. They had slipped into a kind of nonexclusive arrangement that for a while had seemed fine to him. Increasingly, though, he had found himself wondering what she was doing when he wasn't with her.

It had happened almost imperceptibly over a week or two—the shift from something like indifference to the state he was in now, in which he was phoning and messaging her more and more often just to satisfy himself that she was alone. He looked at his watch. It was late afternoon. Low sun shone through a line of palm trees with partially whitewashed trunks. The road ran along the ocean. On a wide beach numerous games of football were in progress on the sand.

Werner noticed that a small crowd had formed near the taxi and people were shouting. He leaned out of the window, trying to see what was happening—and when he was unable to see that way, he opened the door and half-stood. A moped lay on its side, damaged. No one, however, was paying any attention to that. The crowd had gathered around what seemed to be a young man, also lying on the warm asphalt, motionless, and wearing, as far as Werner was able to make out, a pale-blue football shirt. A policeman was there now, in his military-looking uniform, trying to make the crowd stand back and asking questions. He obviously wanted to talk particularly to the taxi driver, and Werner looked at his watch again. If this went on much longer he would need to find another taxi somehow. Traffic was building up behind the incident and filtering slowly past. A blast of wind from the ocean made the palm trees wave and clatter. *"Il est mort,"* Werner heard someone say, someone who had been hanging around on the edge of the crowd and now had to leave, had somewhere to go to.

Werner also had somewhere to go to.

He wondered what to do.

It seemed terrible, in a way, to worry about getting to the airport on time when a boy was lying dead on the road.

It was, he thought, the first time he had actually seen a dead body. Not that he could really see it. He saw the motionless limbs, but he could not see the face, the eyes. There was a dark liquid on the asphalt—it looked too dark to be blood, but that's what it must have been.

The sun was low in the sky and shadows stretched across the road.

The policeman was asking the taxi driver aggressive questions. A few other policemen had also appeared now.

Werner looked at the beach again. He hated beaches. In the distance the oceanic surf was visible as a mass of white spray hanging in the evening air.

When he was five years old, his sister, Liesl, had drowned in the sea.

His earliest memories were of that day, of moving with terrible frantic fear among sun umbrellas and loungers with his father, who was holding his hand painfully tightly. The sand was also painfully hot under his feet, though the overwhelming sense of emergency prevented him from mentioning that as his father almost dragged him along. The place was a small seaside resort in north-eastern Italy. It was popular with families with young children because of the way the water was so smooth and shallow—you could wade out hundreds of meters and it was still only waist-deep.

He wasn't sure which of the images in his head were actual memories of that afternoon, and which were things he had been told in the years since then. Probably most of them were things he was told afterwards, although he had no memory of anyone ever describing that afternoon to him, or talking much about it at all.

He had an idea that, as he and his father hurried over the hot sand, someone started to make an announcement on the public speakers—that a woman's voice, speaking Italian, started echoing metallically in the air. Perhaps he understood that what the voice was saying had something to do with the fact that Liesl was missing, as that was apparently when he said to his father, "I hope Liesl isn't gone, because I love Liesl."

Some years after the event he overheard his father telling someone else that he had said that. Of course, he had no memory of "loving" Liesl, and found it hard to imagine what he might have meant by it. He knew as a matter of fact that for nearly four years they had been together practically all the time, which was strange as he was now unable to remember a single moment of those years, or a single thing that his sister had actually done.

He never saw her again.

When they went home, he was surprised to find that her bed had disappeared from the room they shared.

Even so, it was a long time before he understood that he really would never see her again.

It was a long time as well before he understood that his parents would never be the same again either.

In other words, for a few years he thought that it would be possible to go back to how things were before— that Liesl would somehow reappear, and things would be like they were. It was hard to say at exactly what point he realized that that was never going to happen, that this new situation was one that was going to last forever.

He looked at his watch again. He would need to find another taxi. He stood at the road's edge, trying to flag one down.

The sun was setting and the muezzins were starting up. Each time there was a faint crackle of static and then the voice would launch into the words, the long, stretched-out syllables—*Allahu akbar.*

He was half an hour late to the airport. He apologized and told the captain, who had already started the walk-around when he arrived, that he would explain what had happened later.

They finished the walk-around together and went up the outside steps into the plane, which was an old McDonnell Douglas freighter, strange-looking with its third engine stuck in the tail. Werner would be flying it. At the head of the runway he waited for permission to take off. A voice in his earphones: "Lufthansa Cargo 8262, runway one, cleared for takeoff." "Cleared for takeoff," Werner said back, "runway one, Lufthansa Cargo 8262." The engines spooled up to a high-pitched whine and then delivered their thrust, at which the plane started to move. It picked up speed and when it was traveling at 278 kilometers per hour it took off. Werner always liked to think of the fact that at that moment the plane was unable *not* to take off, that nothing would be able to hold it down.

The ocean slipped under its nose. The blue curve of the planet. Two hours later, they were still ahead of the night. The night was moving faster than they were, though, and overtook them somewhere over the Atlantic. The sky flamed on the western horizon. The ocean winked as the sun fell into it. "Contact now Atlantico." The voice of the air traffic controller, still in Dakar. "Thank you," Werner said. "Good night." The captain, sitting next to him, pointed at the nearly dark and disappearing ocean and said something. There was still a faint light where they were, eleven kilometers up. Werner was thinking that it was night already in Dakar. In Frankfurt it was already night. "This is where it went down," the captain was saying.

"What?" Werner asked, his thoughts elsewhere.

"Air France 447."

Werner peered into the silvery dimness.

"Pretty much on the equator. So what happened?" the captain asked. "Why were you late?"

"There was some sort of accident," Werner said. "A traffic accident."

"Yeah?"

"The taxi I was in hit a scooter," Werner explained. "The kid who was on the scooter was killed, I think."

"Ah shit," the captain said.

"Anyway they had to take the taxi driver away, the police. And I had to get another taxi, which wasn't so easy at that time."

"Sure," the captain said. "That's sad, about the kid."

"Yeah, it is," Werner said. "You know," he said, a minute later, "I had a sister—she died when I was five."

"Yeah?" The captain was obviously unsure what he was meant to do with that information. He and Werner knew each other only slightly and Werner had never told him anything significant about his personal life. "Was she older than you?" the captain asked, trying to show some sort of sympathetic interest.

"No, younger. She was three."

"That must have been hard on your parents," the captain said.

Werner said that it was.

For a while there were no pictures of Liesl in the flat. Later there were some again, and it was strange to see them because by then he had forgotten what she looked like. And of course she still looked the same, in those pictures, while he was already a few years older than he had been that day. That was when he first started to think about what she might look like if she had lived. He still thought about that sometimes—not only about what she might look like, but about what her life might have been like. She would be thirty-three now. When he thought about that, he had an eerie sense of her absence from the world.

From the moment they landed in São Paulo, he dreaded being alone in a hotel room again. He hated the silent solitude of hotel rooms. This one was on the twenty-third floor, with windows that didn't open. He fetched a glass from the bathroom, and the bottle of Wild Turkey he had picked up as he hurried through the airport in

Dakar. He poured some into the glass. And then, even though it was after 2 a.m. in Frankfurt, he tried to phone Sabine again—he tried her knowing that she wouldn't answer. He had tried her many times in the last twenty-four hours, and she had never answered, and now it was the middle of the night where she was. And yet his heart still seemed to stop as the numbers were fed with little flicking sounds into networks that stretched to the other side of the world. Seconds passed, seconds of silence. And then, it felt like some kind of miracle, like something impossible actually happening, her voice was present in his ear, was saying, "Hello Werner."

"You're still up?" was all he said, in surprise. He was looking out at the silent lights of São Paulo, the way they shimmered in the distance, like a mirage.

"Yeah, I'm still up," she said. "How are you?"

"Okay," he told her.

Their talk lasted no more than five minutes, and when it was over he wished he was still in the sky.

4

GRU–YYZ

The next morning she had to lose the pilot before she could leave. He was still in her bed, asleep. "Hey," she said. "Hey. I have to go." He opened his eyes—light blue. There was reddish stubble on his big jaw. He looked around, still not sure where he was. Outside, the last rain of the São Paulo summer was falling, audible in occasional plinks and tinks on the window.

"What time is it?" he finally asked, propping himself up.

"Almost eleven," she told him. "I have to leave in ten minutes."

Looking around in a more focused way now—maybe trying to find his clothes—he wanted to know if he had time for a quick shower.

"Sure," she said. "If you want. But as I say, I have to leave in ten minutes."

Last night, he had wanted to talk a lot first. There was a point when she wondered if talking was all he wanted to do. That happened sometimes. She had swigged from her Heineken and asked him what sort of planes he flew. "The McDonnell Douglas MD-11F," he told her. "The freighter."

"The freighter?" she asked, taking another impatient swig.

They were sitting next to each other on her sofa.

"Yeah."

"What's that like?"

He shrugged. "Not so different from flying passengers," he said.

"Do you do that sometimes?"

"Not anymore."

She had one of those moments when the presence of a large stranger in her apartment suddenly seemed surreal, and for a few seconds even slightly threatening.

"So why'd you switch?" she asked.

He shrugged again. He was perched on the edge of the sofa, as if he wasn't planning to stay long. "I don't know," he said. And then, "The pay's a bit better."

"Better? For flying freight around? Than people?"

"Yah," he said, sort of seeing her point. He tried to explain. "The freight side is more profitable."

"Okay."

"So what do you do?" he asked.

She told him she was a journalist.

He didn't seem sure what to make of that. He said, "So . . . What sort of . . . You write things or . . . ?"

"Well, for instance," she said, "I have to fly to Toronto tomorrow to do an interview."

"Ah," the pilot said. He seemed to be wondering how this affected their present situation. Then he said, "Who are you going to interview?"

She told him—Marion Mackenzie.

She wasn't that surprised when he said he hadn't heard of her.

"She's a pretty famous writer."

"I don't read much," he admitted.

"She's kind of a heroine of mine."

"You must be excited about that then."

"I am."

She was also nervous, and she had wanted something to take her mind off it. That something had turned out to be him. He was what the app had offered her.

When she kissed him, mostly just to end a silence that was starting to turn awkward, he had frozen for a few seconds of startled passivity and then started kissing her back.

While he was in the shower, she looked at her list of interview questions. (He had asked her, politely, whether she had a spare towel. She had fetched one and handed it to him. He had thanked her.) She looked over the list of questions as she waited for the coffee to froth up in the pan. The first question was about whether Mackenzie felt wiser now than when she was younger and . . . The sound of the shower was still going on. She hoped she wouldn't have to knock on the door and tell him to hurry up. She should have made him leave last night, obviously. That she had not done that had something to do with an exchange that happened afterwards, as they lay there sweatily in the dark, each seemingly intent on their own thoughts. He had asked her, unexpectedly, how old she was. "Thirty-three," she said, "like it says on my profile." He was silent for so long that she thought he might have fallen asleep. Then he spoke again. "Are you happy?" he asked. It was a serious question and she tried to answer with the same seriousness. "What is happy?"

"Well, if you had to say whether you were happy or unhappy," he said, "which would it be?"

She thought about it. "I don't know," she said.

There was another long silence, and then he said, "Are you happy that you're alive?"

That was an easier question to answer. "Yes," she said. "I'm happy that I'm alive."

She had let him put his arms around her, and he fell

42

asleep like that, holding her as if she was someone he knew, and though she had slipped out of his embrace, she had not woken him, he was sleeping so quietly. She turned off the gas under the coffee and waited while it simmered down. The sound of the shower was still going on, and she went and knocked on the door. "I have to leave in five minutes." The shower stopped. "I have to leave in five minutes," she said again.

"Okay," his voice said.

There was, she felt, no sense of urgency in it.

"Okay?" she asked.

Nothing.

She went back to the living room, which had the kitchen at one end of it, and poured coffee from the little pan into a mug. She added milk and sugar. She was just lifting the mug to her mouth when she noticed his purple shirt on the floor—that had come off while they were still on the sofa. She put the mug down and took the shirt into the bedroom, where he was unhurriedly toweling his hair. "Here's your shirt," she said.

"Thank you," he said.

There was always something exciting about seeing someone naked for the first time, and his nakedness now, the next morning, still had some of that quality. She felt it as she stood there, her heart perceptibly quickening.

When he took the shirt from her he held on to her hand for a moment. "I have to go," she said.

A few minutes later he appeared in the living room, dressed and looking slightly dazed, as if he still hadn't worked out where he was and what was happening.

She said, "My Uber will be here in a minute."

"Okay." He sat on the sofa and started to put on his shoes. "Where are you going?" he asked. "The airport?"

"Yes."

"Guarulhos?"

"Yes."

"Can I come with you?"

The question seemed weird. "Why?" she asked, making sure she had her passport.

"I need to go there," he said.

"Yeah?"

As he finished tying his shoes he said something about supervising the loading of the plane—the freighter, he must have meant—and offered to pay half the Uber fare. She said that wasn't necessary.

They took the lift down to street level in silence.

Her apartment was in a pale tower, one of several nearly identical ones, next to a highway. The tops of the towers disappeared into cloud and a tangible dampness filled the air outside, where the Uber was waiting—a charcoal Prius slick with moisture.

They got in on opposite sides, and she told the driver to take them to the airport.

They probably seemed like a couple who had just had an argument, she thought—the way they stared out of their windows at the rainy, gray cityscape as it went past. On either side of the highway there was dull warehousing, industrial parks. The traffic was heavy, and she looked at her watch more nervously each time the Uber slowed into another tailback, or arrived just too late at some lights.

At some imperceptible point, as the traffic thickened and their progress slowed, the idea that she might miss the plane started to acquire the qualities of an actual possibility. She leaned pointlessly forward in her seat to look out through the windscreen at the mass of taillights ahead.

The pilot said, "What time is your flight?"

When she told him, he looked at his own watch and said, "It's tight."

"Yeah," she said.

They had stopped again. The driver sighed, as if in apology, though it wasn't his fault, and tapped his fingers on the steering wheel.

"How long is the flight from here?" the pilot asked. "To Toronto. Nine hours?"

"More like ten," she said.

He nodded. "Yah. People are always amazed," he said, "how that part of North America is nearer to, like, *Moscow* than it is to here."

She leaned forward into the space between the two front seats and asked the driver, in Portuguese, whether there was any other way he could go.

He shrugged and said he could try Via dos Trabalhadores. "Why don't you do that?" she said.

"People have no sense of geography," the pilot said. "How the world fits together, you know."

"Yeah," she said.

"Is it Air Canada?" he asked.

"Yes."

"What aircraft do they use on that sector?"

"I don't know," she said.

The traffic had moved on a little and they were now first in line at the next lights.

She said to the driver, "Why don't you turn here? And take Via dos Trabalhadores?"

Without saying anything the driver put his indicator on, and when the lights changed he made the turn, even though he was in the wrong lane. She looked at her watch. Unless they were there in the next fifteen minutes, she thought, she would miss it. She might miss it anyway. She should just accept that she had missed it, she told herself.

A few minutes later, signs for the airport started to appear.

And then a plane, low in the sky, materializing suddenly out of the white vapor. They were nearly there, and she started to think, with something more than mad hope, that she might make the flight after all.

"Will we see each other again?" the pilot asked.

The question surprised her.

"I thought it was fun, last night," he said.

"It was. Sure."

They had to stop for the driver to take a ticket from a machine.

The pilot said, "You know, I never slept with a black girl before."

She laughed, and didn't know what to say. "No?"

"No," he said, smiling at her. "Was my first time."

"Okay," she said. "It's terminal three," she told the driver, after looking it up on her phone. He nodded.

The pilot was saying something about when he would be in São Paulo again.

And then they were there—joining a line of parked taxis in front of the mirrored surface of the terminal.

"Thanks," she said to the driver, jumping out.

The driver more slowly moved round to lift her suitcase from the trunk. She took it from him and thanked him again.

The pilot was standing there, in his purple shirt and his sunglasses, despite the lack of sun.

"Bye," she said. Then she was dragging her suitcase at a half-jog towards the terminal entrance and didn't hear what, if anything, he offered in return.

5

YYZ–SEA

She was very apologetic but she told the interviewer—a young woman who had flown all the way from Brazil—that she had to leave immediately. "My daughter has just gone into labor," she explained. "In Seattle. The only flight they have today leaves in"—she looked at her watch—"exactly two hours. So I have to dash. I'm so sorry."

"Oh," the interviewer said. "Well . . ."

"I'm so sorry," Marion said again, when the woman showed no sign of moving from her sofa.

"Well would it be okay," the interviewer asked, finally standing, "if I e-mailed you some questions?"

"Of course it would. Yes, of course. I'm just going to throw some things in a suitcase," Marion said, and she left the room.

She had been in the middle of answering a question about cultural appropriation when the phone had interrupted her. Something had told her not to ignore it.

51

They parted on the sidewalk in front of the house, with the taxi waiting there, Marion asking if she could give her interviewer a lift, and the interviewer saying that she was fine, thank you.

The only direct flight from Toronto to Seattle that day was on one of the no-frills airlines, which Marion still thought of as a new phenomenon, though they had been around for decades. From her narrow seat, she looked down at what was probably North Dakota. The plane swayed lightly from side to side as she peered at the pale landscape passing slowly underneath. It was hard to tell at times whether the expanse of whiteness she saw was cloud or the surface of the earth, where people actually lived. Sometimes the dark threads of roads gave it away. Marion was able to imagine what it would be like down there. She herself had started life in a place like that. Hard and flat, and hostile to things that lacked obvious utility. There *had* been a library in that small Manitoba town, and she had spent most of her time there when she was in her early teens. People had said of her then that she had her head in the clouds, and it was true that she had liked looking at the sky—that she had often thought it was the only thing worth looking at there.

The plane shook and tumbled over the mountains

and fell through the clouds towards Sea-Tac, from where Marion phoned Doug, while waiting at the luggage carousel. He didn't answer, but phoned her back a few minutes later to tell her the news. As he told her, she was jostled by someone moving forward for their luggage. She didn't notice, even when they swore at her. She said, "Oh Doug. How are they?"

"Okay," he said. She thought he might have sounded happier—no doubt he was in shock, like most first-time fathers.

She told him she would see him soon.

It was still only midafternoon, Pacific time, but the weather, the pouring rain, meant the light outside gave the impression of dusk.

When she arrived, Doug wasn't around. He had gone home for a while, the nurse thought, when Marion presented herself, still with her suitcase, at the maternity department somewhere high up in the hospital. She waited—not taking a seat as she had been invited to—while the nurse went to see whether Annie was awake. The nurse returned and told her that she was. "Put these on, please," the nurse said, offering her what seemed to be a shoebox full of blue shower caps. It took Marion a moment to understand what they were. She sat down to stretch two of them over her shoes. When she had done that, the nurse directed her to a dispenser of disinfectant gel for her hands. Then she said, "Go *down* the hall, second room on your left."

"Thank you," Marion said, and went.

With her heart thumping, she went.

She saw them through the glass panel in the door—Annie sitting up in the bed, with the tiny thing, wearing a onesie that Marion herself had sent, held uncertainly to her chest. Marion paused outside the door, wanting to hold on to this moment of seeing them like that. She wiped a single surprising tear from her eye, and then a second. And then laughed for a moment, silently, at the fact that she was shedding tears. Then she pushed the door open and went in. She was smiling. Annie looked up and immediately said, almost shouted at her, "He's blind."

Marion just stood there.

"They say he's blind," Annie said. "That's what they say."

Marion, stuck in the doorway, was half-aware that she was still smiling.

"That's what they say," Annie said again.

Marion knew she couldn't just stand there.

She had to do something.

She stepped to the bed and took the baby from her daughter. And it was as if she hadn't heard what Annie had said—she felt that herself, that she was just doing what she would have done if Annie hadn't said those things.

"Did you hear what I said?" Annie asked.

"Yes, I heard you."

"And? Don't you have anything to say?"

Marion struggled. Finally she asked, "Does Doug know?"

"Yes. As soon as they told him," Annie said, in tears now, "he left."

"He left?"

"Yes—he left!"

Marion was staring at the hours-old thing in her hands, the red creases in the face that seemed to be made of red creases. The black feathers of hair on the tender skull. She had never warmed to newborns—even Annie had seemed ugly to her when they handed her over. In fact, she didn't like kids much at all. After Annie, she had known she was done. She had had no desire to do it again, any of it. She was staring at the baby's velvety skull and struggling again to think of something to say. "Does he have a name?" she asked finally.

"Thomas," Annie said, with tears sliding down her face.

"That's nice."

Supporting the baby's head, Marion sat carefully down on the chair that was there. He seemed weightless in her hands.

She was very aware of her failure to be equal to the needs of this moment. That her daughter needed something from her was painfully evident. It was also painfully

evident that she didn't seem to have what was needed—
didn't even seem to know what it was.

"I like it," she said, still talking about the name,
though too much time had passed and it wasn't obvious
what she meant. And anyway, it seemed like a useless
thing to say, a thing that simply emphasized the fact that
she had no words that might actually be able to help. She
felt her own insufficiency as a human being, and more
than anything she just wanted to leave—and then she
felt that that desire to leave was also a kind of failure,
and a shameful one, so that it was difficult even to look
Annie in the eye.

When she handed Thomas back to her, she asked, in
a way that still failed to acknowledge what she had been
told, if there was anything that Annie needed.

And yes, there were some things.

Marion, taking her pen out of her handbag, wrote a
neat list.

She wandered the aisles of the supermarket in a daze. She
already knew that the significance of what had just happened would expand as time passed—would expand, in
her own mind, and in Annie's too, into something huge,
into a major failure, of motherhood, of humanity, a
defining event in their lives, from which neither of them

would ever be entirely able to escape, whatever happened in the future. It was one of those events, she thought, that make us what we are, for ourselves and for other people. They just seem to happen, and then they're there forever, and slowly we understand that we're stuck with them, that nothing will ever be the same again. When someone said her name she did not, for a few seconds, understand that they were talking to her. Two women were standing there. They looked Chinese or something. The younger of the two was smiling at her. "Excuse me," she said again. "Are you Marion Mackenzie, the writer?"

Marion had to think about it, she had to take a moment to ask herself whether she was in fact "Marion Mackenzie, the writer." "Yes," she said. "I am."

"I'm such a huge fan of yours," the woman said.

"Thank you," Marion said.

"My name's Wendy."

"Nice to meet you, Wendy."

"Are you okay? You seem very wet," Wendy said, the smile vanishing from her face. Marion was indeed very wet—she was dripping onto the floor and her hair was stuck to her forehead. She had walked for ten minutes through a downpour to get to the supermarket.

"Yes, I'm fine," she said. "I need to buy an umbrella," she added, trying to make light of it.

"Yes, you need one here," Wendy said. And then,

"This is my mom, Jackie." At the sound of her name, the older woman just nodded. She was about Marion's age.

"Hello," Marion said to her tentatively, wondering if she even spoke English.

"She's over from Hong Kong," Wendy said. "She teaches English lit in college there."

"Oh." Marion tried to seem unsurprised, and interested. "Okay."

"She teaches your work, actually."

"Oh yeah? Well. That's . . . very nice. . . ." Marion again looked at the older woman, Jackie, who again merely nodded, and smiled.

Then Wendy said, "Well, it was such a pleasure to meet you."

"You too."

It seemed, at that point, that the encounter was at an end. Wendy, though, had another question—"What are you doing in Seattle?"

"I'm, uh. I'm here to visit my daughter," Marion said, touching her hair, and finding herself momentarily shocked at how wet it was.

"She lives here?"

"Yes, she does."

"Okay," Wendy said, full of enthusiasm. "Would you mind," she asked, "I know you must get this all the time, would you mind signing something for me?" She had her handbag open and was trying to find something, some piece of paper, for Marion to sign.

"Sure," Marion said.

Wendy laughed. "I wish I had one of your books with me." She handed her instead a small notebook and a pen.

Marion wrote her name on the open page of the notebook, and handed the things back.

"Thank you so much," Wendy said.

"Sure."

"You're a wonderful writer."

"Thank you," Marion said, and to Wendy's surprise, she soggily embraced her. "Oh!" Wendy said. "Wow!" Marion, in fact, was very emotional suddenly. With tears in her eyes, she simply nodded at the older woman, Jackie, who taught her work to students in Hong Kong, and then turned and hurried away down the supermarket aisle.

6

SEA–HKG

She woke to the dim stillness of the cabin. This had already happened several times, and each time what she had experienced was less like sleep than like an odd discontinuity in her presence in the world. She woke to the dim stillness of the cabin. Stillness, not silence. There was the sound of the engines—an unvarying sound like a large waterfall somewhere nearby—that muffled all other sounds so that it seemed as if she had stuffing in her ears. It was night and the main lights were switched off. Stretched out on her nearly flat bed, she was able to see, from where her head was, her neighbor's screen. He was watching a film. The silent pictures troubled her—some people shouting at each other—and she shut her eyes again, and thought of the two weeks she had just spent in Seattle with her daughter, Wendy, and her family. They had left her tired, those two weeks, even though they hadn't particularly done much. There had been some little outings—to the Japanese Garden, to the top of the

63

Space Needle. There had been frequent visits to shopping malls and supermarkets. There had been time with the kids, picking them up from school and preparing meals. In Seattle, she had found herself able to forget the situation she was flying back to.

Last autumn she had had a health scare. It had turned out to be a false alarm. Still, it had frightened her. Even when the doctor told her she had nothing to worry about she was obviously shaken and, since it was the end of his working day, he had offered to take her for a drink. "You look like you could use one," he had said. They went to the Conrad hotel, which was near his office. It was pleasant enough. She didn't expect to hear from him again. Then the following week he had invited her to an exhibition of Buddhist sculpture—the subject of this exhibition had been mentioned over their drink, and they seemed to have a shared enthusiasm for it. That was when she first knew that something was happening, the way her heart quickened when she saw that SMS. She told herself that she was a sixty-year-old married woman, that it was absurd for her to feel that kind of excitement over an invitation to an art exhibition, issued in the form of a text message with a link to the exhibition website. The fact was, it felt unmistakably like a date, something neither of them acknowledged when it took place—which it did, after she had spent some days going through the motions of wondering whether to accept the invitation. After that they met a few more times—they went to see films and exhibitions, and then had lunch or a drink.

When she told her husband that she was in love with someone else, he stared at her as if he was literally unable to believe what she had just said.

"Who?" he finally asked.

"It doesn't matter," she said.

"I don't understand," he said.

"Neither do I," she said.

They sat there for a long time in silence. They had been married for nearly forty years and nothing like this had ever happened. There was a feeling, apart from anything else, that it was late in the day for this sort of thing. There was also a feeling of desolation.

"I had to tell you," she said. "We've never hidden things from each other."

"Thank you," he said.

There was another long desolate silence.

He said, "So . . . so you love him?"

"Yes," she said, without hesitation.

"What happens now?" he asked.

"I don't know."

"What do you want?" he asked.

"I don't know," she said again. Though that wasn't true—she knew that she wanted the doctor, who was the only thing she thought about from the moment she woke up in the morning until the moment she finally fell asleep at night.

Her husband sighed.

Strangely, their life went on outwardly as normal for a while after that, though with a kind of silence at the heart of it.

She opened her eyes—the localized lights and silhouettes of the Delta first-class cabin, the shapes of the seats, or pods they were more like, with their semiprivate, semienclosed spaces. She adjusted her position. Her neighbor's screen was still showing the same film. Her own showed a map of their progress—they were eight hours into the flight, and far out over an ocean of unimaginable size. On the map the plane was marked by a plane-shaped symbol that would be, if it were to scale, about a thousand kilometers long. In fact it was hard to understand quite what an insignificant speck this airplane was, in terms of the size of the ocean it was flying over, in terms of the quantity of emptiness that surrounded it on all sides.

In February the doctor had tried to persuade her to spend a night or two away with him. He had suggested Hainan Island, he said he knew some nice places near the sea. That they would sleep together there wasn't explicitly the idea—they had still hardly touched each other—

though they both understood that was probably what would happen. He was more than ten years younger than her and unmarried. When she told him that she was in love with him he had, after a short pause, taken her hand. She had let him take it. Her hand felt hot and damp in his. That was when he first suggested the trip to Hainan. She had said she would think about it.

While she was wondering whether to go to Hainan Island with the doctor, her husband said to her one day, "You have to decide what you want."

"What do *you* want?" she asked him.

"I want you," he said.

"I'm going to Hainan Island next weekend," she said.

"Okay," he said, and his eyes filled with tears.

His quiet acceptance of the situation was mature and fully acknowledged her autonomy as an individual, and she despised him for it.

She didn't know what he should have done.

Nothing, she thought, would have prevented her from going to Hainan Island at that point—it seemed more important than anything else in her life, and worth whatever price life might exact for it.

They went one weekend in early March.

The hotel was near the sea—the windows of their

suite looked onto the ocean. They walked along the sand, the tall surf battering blindly away at the shore.

On the very southern tip of the island, on some wave-lashed rocks, they found a rough brown stone on which was inscribed, in two Chinese characters: *The end of the civilized world.*

The day she got back from Hainan, that Sunday evening, her husband said again, "You have to decide what you want."

She had just stepped into the flat, straight from the airport, the Hainan Airlines luggage tag still on her suitcase. He was sitting there in his pajamas. He didn't look well. He had lost weight, and had stopped shaving every day. And he hadn't been sleeping well—they still slept next to each other, everything was still outwardly the same.

"Okay," she said.

She had a shower and then told him that she was planning to visit their daughter in Seattle for two weeks. When she came back, she said, she would have made a decision.

The map on her screen showed that the plane was flying south now, over the far eastern peninsulas of Russia, towards Japan. In less than five hours it would land in Hong Kong.

It wasn't so much a matter of deciding between her husband and the doctor. It was a matter of deciding whether the fact that she had fallen overwhelmingly in love with the doctor somehow in itself annulled her marriage. Once, when they were much younger, she had loved her husband in something like the way she loved the doctor now. She hadn't thought she would ever love anyone else like that. And now there was the doctor. And it seemed obvious that just as she had stopped loving her husband like that, she would in time stop loving the doctor in that way too. That was the difference—she knew that now. She wouldn't love the doctor in this way forever, so she shouldn't do anything predicated on the idea that she would. And she didn't intend to. Was that maturity? Was it wisdom? Whatever it was, the question insisted on an answer—did the fact that she had fallen in love with the doctor somehow in itself annul her marriage? Did it make it somehow untrue? She did not want to live with something untrue.

Her flight from Seattle landed just after eight in the morning. She took a taxi to the flat, which was in the Mid-Levels, not far from the university where she worked. Her husband was at home. She had not doubted that he would be. When she arrived, he was sitting at the kitchen table in his white squash clothes—he had just returned from his weekly session at the club and still smelled faintly of the sweat he had expended. He was eating fruit salad. She took off her jacket and sat down at the table with him. There were pleasantries, and then some small talk about how things had been in the States, about Wendy and the kids—they hadn't spoken on the phone even once while she was there. When they had dealt with all that, he stood up to make some more coffee and she said, "I don't want to live with something that isn't true."

"What do you mean?" he asked, sitting down again.

"I mean that I don't want to live a life that isn't true. Where we're just going through the motions."

"I don't either," he said.

He looked nice, in his whites. She found herself looking at him as if he was a stranger, someone she didn't know and was seeing for the first time. And in a sense he had become a stranger to her over the past ten weeks. This shift in perspective took her slightly by surprise, the way he seemed positively attractive now, as a sort of stranger in his sweaty shirt, with his lean muscles, and his intelligent eyes, which were trained on her, trying to perceive what it was that she intended or hoped for from this talk. Which in fact was still not entirely obvious to her, though his sudden sexiness—which seemed to have something to do with his now being this semi-stranger with whom things might develop in any number of ways, which after all was what the situation truly was, and always had been—was starting to move things in a particular direction. He felt this and took her hand. She let him do that, as she had let the doctor do it that afternoon when she told him she loved him. As it had that afternoon, her hand felt hot and damp. And as the doctor had that afternoon, he leaned towards her and kissed her mouth, and she let him do that as well. She put her hands on his skin, inside his shirt, and then he was pulling her underwear down to her knees, and there on the kitchen table that morning they tried again to make something true.

7

HKG–SGN

That Friday Dr. Abir Bannerjee left his office early and went to the airport. The weekend of golf with his brother, Abhijit, was something they did every year, usually somewhere inexpensive in Southeast Asia. This time it was Vietnam. From Hong Kong, it was not a long flight—not much more than two hours—and it was only mid-afternoon when he landed in the city he still thought of as Saigon. He sat in the back of the taxi looking out at the noisy, energetic poverty of modern Vietnam. His driver, a talkative fellow though without much English, tried to engage him in conversation, but Abir's monosyllabic answers eventually discouraged him, and they passed the remainder of the journey in silence. For part of that time Abir's thoughts were taken up with someone he knew, a woman he had been seeing. She was married and she had decided, in the end, to stay with her husband. When she had told him that, the previous day, over a drink at the Conrad hotel, he had tried to be philosophical. That was life. He approved of her decision in principle, and he was thankful for what they had had together. For an hour afterwards he had walked the streets, trying to work out how he felt. There was a sort of numbness that made it hard to say. When he wasn't thinking about her, he was mostly thinking about the money his brother owed him—earlier in the year he had lent Abhijit five lakh rupees and he was supposed to have paid it back by now.

The taxi arrived at the Song Be Golf Resort.

It looked, Abir thought, like an upscale Florida shopping mall.

It had been Abhijit's idea to spend a weekend here.

Abhijit himself didn't arrive until later. It was nearly ten o'clock when he thumped on Abir's door. "It's me," he shouted. "Are you asleep or what?" Abir had in fact been thinking of turning in. He was lying on his bed trying to focus on the latest issue of the *Journal of Clinical Oncology*. He put his tablet down, opened the door, and said, "No, I'm not asleep. Hello, Abhijit."

They hugged.

Abhijit smelled of a mixture of sweat and smoke and stale aftershave.

"Drink?" he suggested. "Come on—drink! Let's have a drink. Just one. We can't not have a drink."

Abir let himself be persuaded. He put on his shoes, and they went down to the bar, which was an open-sided area at one end of the lobby level, a sort of veranda, with wicker furniture under turning fans.

"There is no fucking direct flight from India to Ho Chi Minh, can you believe it?" Abhijit said, agitating the ice in his Wild Turkey and Coke.

"There is from Hong Kong," Abir said.

"Yes of course there is from Hong Kong!" Abhijit shouted, enjoying himself. "You can fly fucking anywhere from Hong Kong!" Derisively he threw out the names of some obscure destinations. "Almaty. Port Moresby. Brisbane. Budapest."

"Seattle," Abir added.

"Seattle?"

"Yes, I know someone, she flew in from Seattle a few days ago."

"One of your walking corpses?" Abhijit asked with a jolly laugh.

"No," Abir said. "Not a patient."

"Lucky her." Abhijit slurped from his drink.

"Actually she was a patient," Abir said. "It was a false alarm." He was aware of a desire to talk more about her. "You came via . . . where then? Bangkok?" he asked instead, though he wasn't actually interested in the details of Abhijit's itinerary.

Abhijit nodded. "Sure, yes, Bangkok," he said. "Thai Airways. They're okay." He slurped again from his drink, and patted sweat from his forehead with a napkin—the night was humid. "Are you hungry?" he asked.

Abir shook his head.

They talked for a while about other possible connections—KL, Yangon—and Abir agreed, dispassionately, that the lack of direct flight destinations from India's major airports was a national disgrace.

"The fact is," Abhijit said, "as in so many other areas, we're twenty years behind the Chinese. And you live among them, you traitor!"

"Hong Kong isn't China."

"You're not allowed to say that *there*," Abhijit pointed out.

"Well, you can say anything in India," Abir said. "There is that, on the plus side."

Abhijit frowned. "I'm not sure if that's true anymore actually." He tended his damp forehead. "What did you fly, then?" he asked. "Cathay?"

"No, VietJet," Abir said.

Abhijit seemed amazed. "VietJet? The cheapo outfit? Why?"

Abir shrugged. "It's not a long flight."

There was a silence, and he wondered if this was the moment when Abhijit would bring up the subject of the loan.

Instead Abhijit signaled to an ancient-looking Vietnamese man in a white jacket that he wanted to sign for the drinks.

"I'll get these," he said, and Abir wondered if he expected to be thanked. It did irritate him that Abhijit was making a show of paying for the drinks, was taking the social advantage of that, while at the same time owing him money, and showing no sign so far of being willing or able to pay it back, or even of mentioning it.

"I'll get these," Abhijit said again as the waiter approached, as if Abir might not have heard him the first time.

Abir just nodded and looked away.

"So, what time are we up tomorrow?" Abhijit asked, signing with a flourish, snapping the little padded folder shut, and handing it back to the waiter. "What time are we on the tee?"

Abir did not sleep well. Abhijit's failure to mention the loan needled him for much of the night. He had had a dream in which he was in some vague hotel setting—on an island somewhere—with the woman he had been seeing. Her physical presence had seemed very palpable in the dream, the slightly damp feel of her skin. When he woke up, in the total darkness of the Vietnamese night, he had been surprised for a moment that she wasn't there.

After that he hadn't been able to sleep again for a long time. It was then that he started to think about the money Abhijit owed him. He spent what seemed like hours lying there in the dark, trying to find a form of words with which to approach the subject himself in the morning, if Abhijit did not. He drowsily imagined whole exchanges, some of which ended with Abhijit tearfully apologizing, others with one of them storming out, or even with physical violence. What he did not do was decide on an actual form of words, though he did decide, lying there in the dimness of dawn, that the subject would have to be tackled. Since they were kids, Abhijit's ability to get away with things had infuriated him. He would not let him get away with not even mentioning this loan.

In the morning, however, he ate his fruit salad in silence while Abhijit talked about this and that, about Bitcoin and what fortunes were available there.

"Hasn't it lost, like, half its value in the last few months?" Abir objected.

Abhijit insisted that was a positive sign. He was thinking about making an investment himself, he said as they walked to the first tee.

Abir lost the toss, and stepped up to the tee with his one wood—an undistinguished specimen he had been using since he first took up the sport at Stanford med school.

He tried to empty his mind. He was still thinking

about the loan and it distracted him. It stopped him being fully present in the moment.

Aware that he had lost focus, he stood back from the tee, shut his eyes for a few seconds, and then stepped up to it again.

He inhaled slowly through his nostrils. He made a tiny adjustment to the position of his feet. Then another, which simply undid the first. Then he snapped into the swing, and the little white ball went.

He knew immediately that he had hooked it, though he wasn't sure exactly where it had ended up. The dazzle of the sun had snatched it away.

"Oh dear," Abhijit said, smiling plumply under his Ping visor. "Let's see if I can do any better."

The sun was out, shining down through a thin haze, and they sweated lightly as they stood over their shots. Abhijit had a maddening ability to make the ones that mattered and he was soon several strokes ahead. Abir was obviously out of sorts. He felt the match slipping away as he pathetically missed short putts, then missed them again, and finally sent several shots in quick succession into the weed-filled lake. When the fourth one found the water, he just dropped his iron onto the turf and walked away. "Hey!" he heard Abhijit shouting from the green. "Hey, you need to play a shot. What are you doing? Where are you going? You need to play a shot!" Abir ignored him. He had arrived at a path that led back to the hotel and without thinking he flagged down a resort employee at the wheel of a golf cart that was passing. It was only when he was sitting in the golf cart and it had moved off again under some trees that he was able to take in what he had just done. It seemed incredible that he had actually done it. He never did things like that. As the golf cart trundled along, he found himself thinking of the woman he had been seeing in Hong Kong, of the way she had spoken to him at their final meeting. When she told him her decision, he had been silent for a while. Then he had smiled and said, "Well, I hope we'll still see each other sometimes." And she had said, "No. No we won't."

At the hotel Abir went up to his room and then wondered why he was there. The room had been made up since he was last in it. He sat provisionally on one of the French-style armchairs—perched on it, leaning forward— and stared at the wall. He sat there for some time. Then he went down to the bar, and he was there when Abhijit appeared, dripping from the exertion of finishing the Palm Course on his own. Abhijit sat down and asked the waiter to bring him a large watermelon juice. "What was that about?" he asked, meaning the tantrum.

"Nothing," Abir said.

"Are you okay?" Abhijit patted his face with a napkin.

"When are you going to pay me that money?" Abir asked.

"Money?"

"The five lakh rupees."

"Oh that."

"Yes, that. Were you hoping I'd just forget about it?"

The tone was so hostile that Abhijit, perhaps taken aback, said nothing for a few seconds. Then he said, "Are you okay, Abir?"

At that moment his huge watermelon juice arrived and he let the waiter place it on the table and thanked him, and then asked him for an ashtray.

As soon as the waiter moved away, Abir said, "When are you going to pay me?"

"I think you need to calm down," Abhijit said.

"Don't tell me to calm down. When are you going to pay me?" Abir seemed in danger of losing his temper again.

"What's the matter with you?" Abhijit said.

"When are you going to pay me?"

"What's your problem?"

"When are you going to pay me?"

"It's only five lakh rupees—"

"When are you going to pay me?"

"I'm going to pay you," Abhijit said. "I *am going* to pay you. Okay? What the fuck is your problem?"

8

SGN–BKK–DEL

The first thing Abhijit did, when he arrived back in Delhi on Monday afternoon, was look in on his father. He visited the old man every few days. It was important to him that he did that. The taxi stopped outside the house in Daryaganj. It was the house in which Abhijit had spent part of his childhood, and it was in a dilapidated state now. The turquoise tiles of the façade were falling off, leaving squares of rough cement. A broken window was patched up with plastic sheeting. The metal front door was openly rusting. The old man refused to spend money on maintenance, let alone renovation. Abhijit told the taxi driver to wait and walked through the sultry, particulate fug to the three steps, also shedding their tiles, that went up to the rusty door. He had his own key and he let himself in. Inside, he took off the surgical mask he was wearing. The walls of the narrow hall were lined with what seemed, in the dim light, to be school photos.

Anita was preparing the old man's tiffin in the kitchen. Anita was the day nurse, a young woman from Kerala. Panting from the stairs, and still in his sweaty traveling outfit, a dark-blue Adidas tracksuit, Abhijit asked her how his father was. She said he was fine. Then she said she needed to ask Abhijit for a favor. "Oh yes?" Abhijit said, looking pleased to hear that, smiling at her. He put his hand on her shoulder and said, "What? Tell me."

Her shoulder twitched and he withdrew his hand. He also more or less stopped smiling. She said, "I need to go away for a few days. If that's possible."

"Yes?" he said. "Why?"

Her sister's house in Kochi, she told him, had been destroyed in a fire. She felt she was needed there.

"I see," Abhijit said. "Well, let me think about it."

She started to say something about how it was important that she went as soon as possible.

"Let me think about it," Abhijit said. "You're needed here as well. Is there any mail?" She said there was, and went to get it, while he waited.

There were half a dozen letters, mostly about money in one way or another. Abhijit squeezed each of them with his fingers, as if feeling for something inside, and then put one of them in his pocket. The others he put in a drawer. Anita was still standing there. "Okay," Abhijit said. "I'll see him now."

The old man spent his days in the large room on the east side of the house. He was dressed, as usual, in a shalwar kameez and European-style slippers lined with worn-out, discolored, odorous sheepskin. With his white mustache, he still looked distinguished and slightly fierce, though there was also something fearful, something almost like suppressed panic, about the way he stared up from the wheelchair at Abhijit as his son stood over him and said, "How are you, pitajee?"

The old man made a shaky movement with his hands, the meaning of which was difficult to interpret.

Music was playing. The jingle-jangle harpsichord stuff that the old man had always liked. Abhijit had always hated it. He went to the stereo and turned it down until it was almost inaudible.

"I've been out of town," he explained. "For a few days. That's why I haven't been to see you. I told you about it. I was in Vietnam, playing golf with Abir."

"Abir?"

"Yes." Abhijit smiled, perched on the ottoman now.

It wasn't entirely clear whether the old man knew who Abir was. He looked worried, like an actor who has forgotten his next line. It was true that he hadn't seen Abir for some time. Abhijit tried to think of the last time his brother had been in Delhi. Their mother's funeral, probably, five years ago. He had had to turn up for that.

"It's dangerous there, isn't it?" the old man said.

"Where, pitajee?"

"Vietnam."

"Why's that?"

There was an uneasy silence.

Abhijit guessed what his father was thinking. He said, "The war finished long ago, pita. It's not like that now. It's a popular tourist destination. I was playing golf. With Abir."

"Abir?"

"Yes."

As if passing judgment on an insignificant pupil at the school where he had been headmaster for nearly forty years, the old man said, "A pompous boy. I never liked him."

"Abir?"

"I never liked him."

It was hard to know how to take that. After a few moments, Abhijit said, "Don't be silly, pitajee. He's so like you. He's very smart."

The old man might have been thrown by the Americanism. He said, as if allowing something, and something quite important, "Yes, well. He was always well turned out."

"He still is," Abhijit said. "Very well turned out. He

has impeccable taste. He inherited that from you as well, babu."

"He died?" the old man asked.

"Abir? No. No, he's not dead. I just spent the weekend playing golf with him."

"Ah."

"I won," Abhijit added, unable to stop himself. He felt like a kid, the way he said it, and immediately wished he hadn't. At the same time he was disappointed when the old man didn't seem to have heard him.

The old man leaned in so that Abhijit was able to smell his sticky mouth, and said, "That nurse. She steals from me."

"Pita. I'm sure that isn't true. She's very nice."

"She steals from me," the old man insisted.

"What does she steal?"

"My French pen."

"The Mont Blanc?"

"The French pen."

"Why do you think she stole it?"

"It's not here."

"It's here somewhere."

"No."

"I'm sure it is."

"No."

"Did you look everywhere?"

"Yes."

"Are you sure?"

"It's not here!"

"Please don't make a kerfuffle about this, pitajee," Abhijit said. "The pen will turn up."

Still, he found Anita and said to her, "Have you seen my father's pen? The Mont Blanc. He says it's missing." The tone in which he said it more or less amounted to an accusation and she met his look with a palpable anxiety in her eyes—and also a sort of defiance, which might mean anything. "No," she said. "I haven't seen it."

Abhijit was looking straight at her. "Do you know the one I mean?" he asked. "It has an inscription on it. Something to do with the Minto Academy."

"I haven't seen it," she said again.

He told her that he had some things to do and would be back in an hour.

In the hall downstairs, standing in the semidarkness, he made sure he had what he needed. Then he went out. When he opened the metal door daylight fell into the hall for a few seconds, lighting up the framed school photos on the walls, the mass of young faces under the made-up escutcheon, and the fearsome, mustached headmaster in the middle of the front row. Outside, the taxi was still waiting, and Abhijit got in. He and Abir had both been pupils at the school, a neoclassical building in a mangrove swamp. One day when Abir was about ten, he had been sent to the headmaster by his form teacher for some misdemeanor. The headmaster, of course, was Abir's own father. If Abir had expected this to make any difference to the way he was treated, he was soon disabused of the idea—the headmaster, after reading the note from the form teacher, and addressing his son by his surname even in the privacy of his study, simply asked "Bannerjee" to put out his hands, palms up. What happened next was predictable enough. Then, with tears of pain in his eyes, "Bannerjee" was enjoined to improve his discipline, and dismissed. It was possible that their father later regretted the way he had behaved that day—though no doubt his main concern had been that as headmaster he should not unfairly favor his own sons—because when, a few years later, Abhijit in turn was sent to see him, he had a different experience. The headmaster, addressing him by his first name, acknowledged that Abhijit was his son, and did not inflict physical pain, instead assigning him the more lenient and impersonal punishment of a week of "sanctions"—early morning manual labor alongside the gardeners in the grounds.

———

Abhijit sat in the back of the taxi as it bumped and honked its way through the streets, struggling to make progress. Vehicles of all kinds fought for their share of the filthy asphalt, shoving themselves forward, forcing other people to let them in. Abhijit swabbed his brow with a damp paper tissue, a Thai Airways napkin he had pocketed on the plane. He was sweating unpleasantly— the taxi had no air-conditioning, or if it did the driver wasn't using it to save petrol. Abhijit told him he would pay him extra if he put it on, and after a few seconds the milder air arrived, along with a moldy smell. Abhijit felt the sweat start to dry on his forehead. He had put one of his father's letters in his pocket. Now he took it out and opened it. Inside was a new debit card, stuck to a folded sheet of paper.

The taxi pulled up outside an HSBC bank, and waited while Abhijit, wearing his surgical mask, went to the ATM under its red-and-white-striped plastic awning and withdrew the maximum daily amount. He pushed the wad of money into his wallet as he took his seat in the taxi again and told the driver, who was also wearing a surgical mask, to take him back to his father's house.

He wondered what to do about the Mont Blanc pen. He hadn't expected the old man to notice that it was missing. He wasn't sure what to do about it now. He could just quietly put it back. Or he could let his father think that Anita had taken it. It would give him some kind of hold over her, if she was suspected. Which might have its uses. She had been doing something on her smartphone when he had spoken to her earlier. She had been messaging someone. He wondered who it was, whether it was a man. He knew she wasn't married. He still hadn't decided what to do when he arrived at the house again and let himself in through the rusty door. He went past the school photos and up the stairs.

He had put the debit card back in its envelope and was just putting the envelope in the drawer with the other papers when he heard a noise behind him.

He shut the drawer and turned.

It was Anita.

"What is it?" he said.

For a few seconds she didn't say anything, and he was about to ask her again what she wanted when she said, "I found this." She was holding something—a letter, which had been opened.

"What is it?" he asked.

Again she didn't say anything, and there was something meaningful about her silence now.

Abhijit took the letter from her and saw that it was from HSBC, addressed to his father. He pulled it partly out of the envelope. It was a statement for the previous month. Apart from the usual automatic payment to the nursing agency, there were a number of other transactions. They were all the same. Withdrawals from ATMs, one or two a week, each for the maximum daily amount. "I need to go away for a few days," Anita said.

9

DEL-COK

Kochi airport depressed Anita. Everything about it depressed her. It was nearly ten years since she had moved to Delhi. She had been nineteen, and something had impelled her to leave. She hadn't even been sure what that thing was at the time—she had experienced it only as an inarticulate need to get away—and now, as she always did when she came back, when she passed through the low-ceilinged airport, she experienced a feeling like dread, as if this place might somehow have the power to reclaim her. It was Wednesday afternoon. The sun shone down through glinting clouds. Fanning herself with the magazine she had been reading on the plane, she joined the queue at the auto-rickshaw stand in front of the terminal.

Her sister's house, it turned out, had not actually been destroyed. It didn't even look seriously damaged. After what Nalini had told her on the phone, she had expected a smoldering wreck. So there was a shiver of irritation when she leaned out of the auto-rickshaw and saw that the house looked essentially fine. Part of her wasn't entirely surprised—Nalini wanted her there, and had said what was necessary. As she took out her wallet and extracted a five-rupee note she was angry with her sister, and didn't intend to hide it.

Then she saw her face.

She said, "What's that? He didn't hit you? Tell me he didn't hit you. Please tell me he didn't hit you."

They went inside—the interior of the house was a single room—and sat on chairs facing each other, their knees nearly touching. The chairs were made of bright-orange molded plastic, and had once furnished a snack bar.

"What happened?" Anita said. "Tell me what happened."

The mark on Nalini's face was under her left eye, and the way it swelled out looked painfully tender, as if even the draft from the open door might make it hurt.

"Nothing," Nalini said. "It's okay."

"It's not *nothing*. It's not *okay*. What happened? When did he get here?"

"Last night."

Nalini's husband worked in Qatar, worked as a gardener for a white woman there, apparently.

"His flight got here in the middle of the night," she said.

She kept turning to look at the doorway as if expecting him to appear. Her daughter, Sarah, was standing there, in the doorway. She was fourteen and had a faint black mustache. She didn't seem to be listening to what they were saying.

Nalini said, "And when he saw the house wasn't totally destroyed he got angry."

"You told him the house was totally destroyed?"

"I told him there'd been a massive fire. You didn't see it. It was terrifying."

"I'm sure it was, darling," Anita said. She looked again at the black scorch marks on the ceiling and the floor and tried to imagine the flames that had made them. Some furniture had been damaged too, and was piled up outside. The bedding was hanging up out there as well, to try to get the smell of smoke out of it. There wasn't much left in the room. On one wall was a picture of Jesus, a European-looking man with long silky hair, his heart visible in his chest and emitting rosy light. Some flakes of soot were stuck damply to the picture.

"It was terrifying," Nalini said again.

"So he was angry?" Anita asked. "When he saw the house?"

"He started shouting at us," Nalini said. "It was the middle of the night and he was shouting at us, waking up the whole street."

Anita was able to imagine it. Nalini's husband had

trashed the house in the past. Anita had always been nervous around him. She thought of him, in fact, as a potential murderer, and feared for her sister's safety when he was there, which was normally only once every two years. She nodded.

"And after waking up the whole street, and terrifying the kids, and throwing the furniture around," Nalini said, "he just disappeared. I don't know where he went. It was still the middle of the night. I don't know where he slept."

"Is that when he hit you?" Anita asked. "Last night?"

"No," Nalini said. "That was this morning."

Anita glanced at her niece, still standing in the doorway, and wondered whether she should be hearing this. She thought maybe she would try to talk to her later, alone. She felt a kind of kinship with the silent girl, who in some ways reminded her of herself when she was that age. She wanted to help her. She wanted to make sure she was able to do what she wanted with her life. She wanted, more than anything, to make sure she understood that that was possible. "So he came back this morning?" Anita asked.

"Yes."

"And then what happened?"

"At first he was okay," Nalini said. "He ate something, he had breakfast with us. He even took the kids to school. He'd never seen her school." She nodded towards her daughter. "And then he came back here and looked at the furniture that was damaged. That's when he got angry again, looking at the furniture, telling me how it was my fault it was damaged. He started shouting at me about how much his plane ticket cost to come here. One lakh rupees, he said."

"No," Anita murmured. "That sounds too much."

"That's what he said."

It was cool inside the house, where the walls were painted greenish-blue. The floor was concrete, a complex map of cracks and discolorations.

"And I said I wanted him to come back and live with us," Nalini said, looking Anita in the face. "I told him I couldn't cope on my own, that's why the fire happened. And he said he thought I started the fire on purpose to make him come back. I told him I'd never do a thing like that but I did want him to come back. I said I wanted him to come back and live here. I said that's what I wanted, for him to come back and live here. And he started yelling at me to stop saying that. But it's what I want, I said. That's when he hit me."

Anita waited for a few moments, looking at the swollen place on her sister's face. She thought her husband probably had a woman in Qatar, that was why he was so determined to stay there. She didn't say that. She said, leaning towards her sister so that their noses were almost touching, "There's a phrase for this now. It's 'toxic masculinity.'" She said the words in English, and Nalini didn't understand them, so she tried to find a Malayalam equivalent. "That's what they call it now. And you can't just take it," she said. "You can't. Okay?"

Nalini looked sullen.

She let Anita squeeze her hand, without squeezing back.

"Okay?" Anita said again.

She wondered what Nalini's friends would say about this, what advice they would have for her. Probably something along the lines of *That's what men are like, that's just how they are, he'll leave again soon, why provoke him, what's the point?* Anita had grown up with women like that, and Nalini was the same. "So what am I supposed to do?" she asked.

"Well I think you should leave him," Anita said.

She said it quietly, almost whispered it, aware of her niece still standing in the doorway.

The fact that she had just a week ago ended her own attachment to an objectionable man made her feel more authoritative in saying it. Though Raj, who managed the IT department of an airline, was obviously incapable of physical violence. Perhaps that was only because he had so much more to lose than her sister's husband did, and so many other ways of projecting power in the world. Still, it was impossible to imagine him hitting her. Nalini knew nothing of her five-year affair with him. She would have been shocked by it, Anita thought. That he had been twenty years older than her, and married, and a Hindu— all of it would have shocked her sister deeply. That was a different world, one that she would not understand. So Anita had never mentioned it.

She moved uneasily on her orange plastic seat, still waiting for Nalini to respond to what she had said—*I think you should leave him.*

From the wall Jesus stared blankly at them sitting there, his silky head enclouded in a puff of gold mist. Under the picture were the words *Dona Nobis Pacem.*

"I think you've got to," Anita said. "There has to be some sort of consequence. He can't just get away with doing something like that. And it isn't the first time. I know it isn't."

It was impossible to say, at that point, what Nalini was thinking. She was looking at her own hands, at her intertwined fingers. She was only two years older than Anita but her hands looked twenty years older. She seemed deep in thought, and Anita was hopeful that her words might have had some impact. She felt that she had to make her sister see the importance of not just accepting things as they were as somehow inevitable. She had to make her see the importance of exerting some sort of positive agency in the world. It was the passivity, more than anything else, that infuriated her. "He'll still have to send money for the children," she said, thinking this might be her sister's main worry. "And if he doesn't," she added, "I will."

Even then, Nalini didn't look at her.

And then they heard her son's voice—he had been playing in the sand in front of the house—shouting, "Achan! Achan!"

They heard the man say something to him, without being able to make out what it was.

Anita, her pulse quickening, wondered whether he even knew she was there.

He appeared as a silhouette in the doorway. The boy was jumping about excitedly behind him. "Ammayi Anita is here! Ammayi Anita is here!" he was shouting, as if his father would be as happy about it as he was.

He didn't seem to be.

"What're you doing here?" he asked, pushing his daughter out of the way so that he could advance into the room.

Anita stood up. Her chair made a scraping noise on the floor. "How dare you hit my sister?" she said. And when the man just stared at her, she said again, "How *dare* you?"

She had never been looked at, she thought, with more hatred.

She was shaking.

She wondered if he might be about to attack her. She felt his potential for violence. She saw it in his face, with its thick mustache and its shine of sweat, and it frightened her. She said, "She's going to leave you."

And immediately she heard Nalini's voice, strident in objection, saying, "I'm not."

The man didn't look at his wife. He kept staring at Anita. He stood there for another second or two—long enough for Nalini to say again, "I'm not"—then he turned and left, stopped for a moment to spit pointedly on the dirt outside the house, and walked away, with his son following him, asking what had happened.

10

COK-DOH

The flight landed in Doha just after dawn. For a short time, the sky was a delicate shell-pink and the world looked mild from the window of the plane as it taxied. Shamgar knew this hour. It was the only hour of the day when it was a pleasure to be outside, and he always was outside, stooped over some plant, with fragrant fragments of soil stuck to his hands. He had been in Kochi for five days and he had missed his garden. It wasn't his in the sense that he owned it, of course. It was his in the sense that it had been entrusted to him, that he was the person who knew it most intimately, who understood it most precisely, and who probably loved it the most. Mrs. Ursula sometimes told him to do things—to put in or take out this or that particular plant—but mostly she let him decide what to do.

Shamgar was thankful to have work that he liked, part of the time anyway—there were other tasks he had to attend to, such as washing the cars and the outdoor fur-

niture, and sweeping the swimming-pool area, and looking after the pool itself, lifting leaves and dead insects
and other floating things from its surface every morning
with a fine-mesh net on a long pole. He worked from
six in the morning till six in the evening—from sun-
rise to sunset—with two hours off in the heat of the day
from April to September. Every Sunday morning he also
had two hours off to go to the St. Thomas Syro-Malabar
Church, and every two years he had a month's leave to
visit his family in India.

Mrs. Ursula was his "sponsor," as they said here—
which meant, more or less, his owner. She kept his passport and his work permit, and he was unable to travel
anywhere or do anything without her express permission. She was the dominant figure in his life, and he was
lucky with her, he was aware of that. She paid him more
than most men earned for the sort of work he did—
about a hundred dollars a month—and she treated him
fairly, kindly even. When he told her that his house in
Kochi had been destroyed in a fire, it was she who had
said he must go there immediately, and she who had lent
him the money for his airfare. She said he could pay her
back ten dollars a month for the next three years. "Thank
you, Mrs. Ursula," he said.

While he was away, someone had to water the plants
twice a day—in the early morning and in the evening—

and Shamgar had arranged for the man who worked in the house next door to do it. The man's name was Krish.

When Shamgar arrived at the compound it was mid-morning. The brittle seedpods of frangipani trees broke under his feet as he walked, and the trees themselves were still in flower. The simple five-petaled flowers showed creamily against the glossy darkness of the leaves. There were stretches of shade under the trees, and areas of spongy grass in front of the houses. There were three models of house—small, medium, and large. Mrs. Ursula had one of the medium ones.

As he approached, Shamgar saw immediately that Krish had not done the watering properly. With a painful sense of having been let down, he went to his room, which was a sort of shed on the other side of the house, at one end of the swimming-pool area, up against the wall that separated the property from the one next door. From the outside, with its tiny window, it looked like a storeroom—and indeed the equipment for maintaining the swimming pool was stored in there. He dumped his stuff, and then went out again and attached the hose to the standpipe in the garden.

While he was going around with the hose, directing the flow of water with his thumb, Mrs. Ursula stepped out into the shade of the porch holding a mug and wearing sunglasses. "Hello Shamgar," she said.

He nodded.

She asked him about the situation in Kochi. He told her that things were okay. The house, it turned out, was only slightly damaged.

"I'm very happy to hear that," she said.

So actually it hadn't been necessary for him to go there after all, he said.

He saw her straining to make out what he was saying. His accent, when he spoke English, was very strong. Sometimes he had to say things two or three times before she understood him.

"Well," she said, finally catching the gist of it. "I think it was important that you went anyway, Shamgar. I think that was important. How's your wife?" she asked.

"She's fine, Mrs. Ursula," he said.

"It must have been a tough time for her. She must have been happy to have you around."

He didn't say anything, and after a minute she asked him to please wash her car when he was finished watering the plants. Then she went inside and shut the door. Shamgar had never been inside the house. The housework was done by a man called Manoj who was there for a few hours every day.

———

It was early afternoon. Very hot. He was lying on his bed, lying on his back with one arm under his head, staring at the ceiling. All around him the blue plastic pool equipment was piled up. The air conditioner whirred noisily. It made strange knocking sounds sometimes. It was an old unit. Still, he was thankful to have it. His quarters consisted of a small bedroom with a single window, quite high up, and a tiny bathroom with a shower, a sink, and a toilet. The window looked into the narrow paved space at the side of the house, at the other end of which was the carport.

At about two o'clock he had a shower. The water came from a tank on the roof and, being exposed to the sun, it was almost too hot. There was no cold water, except for a few months in the winter. When he had showered, he put on fresh clothes. Standing in front of the cracked mirror he trimmed his mustache with a pair of nail scissors. The mirror had been in one of the bathrooms in the house. When it had been accidentally broken Mrs. Ursula had suggested that he might like it. He had a last look at himself. Then he went out.

There was, at that hour, a profound stillness everywhere. He left the swimming-pool area by the back gate, walked a little way along the neglected path behind the houses, and entered the swimming-pool area of the neighboring property. He made sure that the carport was empty. Then he tapped on the back door of the house. After waiting for a few seconds, he opened it and went in. The door, which was on a spring, snapped shut. Inside the house the air felt dramatically frigid and dry. Shamgar went through the kitchen and into the dining room where he found Krish sitting at the table.

"What happened with the watering?" Shamgar asked him.

"I did it."

Shamgar wondered what to make of that. He hated the idea that Krish might lie to him. "Looked like it hadn't been done for at least a day," he said. "When'd you last do it?"

"Yesterday morning," Krish said. He was polishing silver.

"That's what it looked like. Why not yesterday evening?"

"I thought you got back yesterday," Krish said, dabbing the grubby chamois in the tin of polish on the table. "Didn't you get back yesterday?"

"No," Shamgar said, "I got back today. This morning."

"I thought you got back yesterday," Krish said.

Shamgar tried not to show how much it upset him that Krish thought he had been back for a whole day and had made no effort to see him. "Why didn't you answer my text?" he asked.

Krish smiled slightly, no doubt thinking of the text that Shamgar had sent him in the middle of the night. He said, "I was planning to. I've been working all day."

"That's no excuse." Shamgar put his hands on Krish's shoulders and felt the warmth of them through the thin shirt he was wearing. "It only takes a minute," he said. When Krish said nothing, Shamgar squeezed his neck. He shoved his fingers through his thick fur-like hair and then took hold of it and pulled, quite hard. "It only takes a minute," he said again.

He had pulled Krish's head back until he was looking up at him, into his eyes, and he was about to lean down and kiss him on the mouth when they heard a sound from the front door, the tentative scratching of a key. For another second they looked into each other's eyes—there was alarm there now, and a sort of excitement too—then Shamgar let go of Krish's hair and walked silently towards the kitchen. He slipped out of the house, taking care to ease the back door shut without a sound, and traversed the swimming-pool area, turning only once to confirm the presence in the carport of the large white SUV belonging to Krish's sponsor.

He lingered on the path behind the houses.

Krish's sponsor—an Australian man—usually didn't appear until much later in the afternoon.

Shamgar wondered whether to go back and see if the car was still there. Possibly the man had just returned home to pick something up, and would soon be gone again.

Shamgar lingered on the path. It still hurt him that Krish thought he had been back since yesterday and had made no effort to see him. If the situation were reversed he knew that he would have been unable to think of anything other than the hour of Krish's return—which he would have known precisely—and that he would have hurried to see him at the first opportunity. It was that knowledge, more than anything else, and the strange painful anger it stirred in him, that stopped him going back.

Instead he walked slowly along the path and pushed open the gate to the swimming-pool area of Mrs. Ursula's house.

Unexpectedly, Mrs. Ursula herself was there, lying on a sun lounger in the shade of the umbrella. She was fully dressed but had pulled her skirt up to the middle of her thighs. At the squeak of the gate she looked up. Her face was flushed. "Oh, it's you, Shamgar," she said.

"Mrs. Ursula."

"Where were you?" she asked.

"I went for a walk," he said. He had to say it a few times before she understood. Then she said, "A walk? Now? It's a bit hot for that isn't it?"

"Yes, Mrs. Ursula," he said.

They were talking across the blue corner of the swimming pool. Bougainvillea blossoms floated on the water like scraps of pink tissue paper. They moved slowly across the surface, carried by the unseen currents of the circulation system.

Mrs. Ursula frowned, as if she didn't understand something, and then shut her eyes again.

After a few moments Shamgar went into his little room and lay on the bed, listening to the knock and squeak of the air conditioner. All he was able to think about was whether Krish would appear there after dark, and what would happen if he did. With what sounded like a sort of urgency, the air conditioner squeaked more and more loudly and then was suddenly quiet. Father Shobi, the priest at the St. Thomas Syro-Malabar Church, would be saddened, Shamgar knew, by the thoughts he was having.

11

DOH–BUD

"My gardener," Ursula said. "You remember my gardener—Shamgar?"

"Yes," Miri said. "Sort of."

"I think he might be gay."

"Yeah? Why?"

Ursula laughed. "I think he might be having some sort of affair with the man who works next door."

"Good for him," Miri said. She didn't seem very interested—her mind seemed elsewhere. Still, Ursula went on with it. "Once I saw the man from next door coming out of Shamgar's room very early in the morning. I hadn't been able to sleep and I was up before dawn and I'd just stepped outside when the door of Shamgar's room opened—and I expected it to be Shamgar of course, but it wasn't. It was this guy from next door. I don't even know his name. 'Oh, hello,' I said. And he just nodded and hurried off. And when I mentioned it to Shamgar later he was *very* embarrassed. I didn't pursue it."

"It's none of your business," Miri said.

"I know. Of course it isn't. He is *married* though. Shamgar. He has two kids back in India. I think the other guy's married as well."

"I'm getting married," Miri said. "What do you feel like?" she asked, picking up the menu. "What's the special today?"

They were in Menza, a popular restaurant near her flat in Budapest. Ursula had arrived on the early flight from Doha and had taken a taxi straight there. She said, "No, Miranda, what do you mean you're *getting married*?"

"I am."

"To someone I know?"

"Yes."

"Who?"

"Who d'you think?"

"To Moussa?"

"Yes."

Miranda, when her mother said nothing else, finally put down the menu. "You could at least pretend to be pleased."

"I'm pleased," Ursula said. "I'm surprised."

"I can see that. Why?"

"It just seems sudden. You and . . . and Moussa have been seeing each other for how long? Not that long."

"More than a year," Miri said.

"Is it that long?"

"Yes."

"Well," Ursula said, "still."

"What do you mean? Is that not long enough? How long do you think *is* enough? Two years? Five? Ten? How long had you and Dad known each other before you decided to get married? Twenty minutes?"

"About four months. And look how that worked out."

"I know how it worked out. I did the therapy. Let's face it," Miri said. "You're surprised because of who he is."

"No," Ursula immediately insisted. And then, "What do you mean?"

"You know what I mean."

"The fact that he's a Muslim," Ursula said, "has nothing to do with it."

"To do with what?"

At that moment the waiter asked them what they wanted to drink. They ordered some fizzy water and asked for a few more minutes to look at the menus.

Which they did, making suggestions to each other over the tops of them, and narrowing down the possibilities, until the waiter was there again and they ordered.

"Look," Ursula said, in German again—they had spoken English to the waiter—"if this is what you want to do, of course I'm pleased. Of course I am."

"But," Miri prompted.

"But nothing. When did he ask you to marry him?" She made the question sound like a matter of minor interest, and as if she had already accepted the major fact, and took a sip of water as she waited for the answer.

"He didn't," Miri said. "It was my idea."

Ursula tried to sound unfazed. "Okay."

"*He* would never ask *me*," Miri said. "He'd understand how that might look."

"How might it look?"

"Like he wanted something. Like it might help him stay in Europe. I don't know."

"Well it might," Ursula pointed out.

"Yes, it might. So? Isn't that a good thing?"

"Is that what this is about?" Ursula asked.

"No," Miri said. "That's not what it's about."

After lunch they took Ursula's suitcase to Miri's flat, which was in a quiet, dirty street on the other side of the avenue. The buildings of the street looked ominously fortified. They stopped at a huge wooden door, in which there was a smaller door. A row of plaster faces, caked with smut, alternately laughed and cried on the building's façade, one under each of the windows of the first floor. The façade itself might once have been turquoise. Now it was a sickly gray. Miri punched some numbers into a keypad and they went through the smaller door and into a tall courtyard under a distant square of sky.

"This is where you live now, is it?" Ursula asked, taking in their surroundings—the silo of silent doors and windows above them, and only a pigeon or two in evidence.

"It's where we live," Miri said.

"He lives here too?"

"Yes."

"Oh," Ursula said. The last thing she had heard, Moussa lived in a precarious semilegal flat-share with some other Syrians. "Is he here now?" she asked.

"Don't think so," Miri said.

Ursula had only met Moussa twice. He was quite handsome, obviously intelligent, humorous, sweet—there was nothing to object to. Except that his very pleasantness seemed suspect, somehow. It seemed implausible that such an appealing person had no existing ties in life. He was in his early thirties, about ten years older than Miri. Ursula wanted to ask her daughter how she could be sure that he didn't have a family back in Syria—a wife, kids, whatever. There was no way of knowing. Ursula had thought about it just that morning on the plane from Doha. There used to be a time when flights from the Gulf to Europe flew over Iraq and Syria—that was the shortest way—only now they had to avoid the sky over those places and fly over Iran and Turkey instead.

127

She had watched, on the seat-back screen, her own flight do just that this morning, divert around Syria and Iraq, and she had thought of Moussa, of course, and of his unknown life down there, in that secret place—a place so secret that it wasn't even possible to fly over it and look at it from ten thousand meters up. What had he left behind there? What ties did he still have? Impossible to say. Look at Shamgar, she had thought, picking at her Qatar Airways breakfast. People were able to live multiple lives.

There seemed no way of putting this to Miri, though.

She did ask her, as they walked through the streets after leaving her luggage at the flat, what she knew about his life in Syria.

"Quite a lot actually," Miri said.

"He's a vet?" Ursula asked.

The question seemed to irritate Miranda. "You know that," she said.

Yes, Ursula knew that.

He wasn't working as a vet in Hungary, of course—his asylum-seeker status prevented him from working officially and what he actually did was teach private Arabic lessons, mostly to postgrad students at CEU, who mostly took them as an act of solidarity. That was how Miri had met him.

They had arrived at the Danube. Ursula stopped for a

moment to take in the view—the hills piled up on the far side of the water with their spires and turrets. Overhead the sun was breaking whitely through clouds.

They set off across the windy bridge. In the middle a subsidiary section swung down to one side, providing access to Margaret Island. The trees of the island were still more or less leafless, but massed together they displayed a sort of green haze that dwindled down the river to another large bridge just visible in the distance.

"What else do you know about him?" Ursula asked.

"How much do you ever know about somebody?" Miri said.

Ursula wasn't having that. "Plenty, after a while. Has he been married before?" she asked.

"No," Miri said.

Ursula had not taken all that much interest in the man previously—she had assumed that Miri's thing with him—and that was how she had thought of it, as an undefined "thing"—wouldn't last long. With that safely assumed, she had in fact found herself feeling cautiously proud of it. That her daughter was involved with a Syrian refugee did no harm to Ursula's liberal bona fides, and she had on occasion more or less shown off about it to a particular section of her friends, though she had always been careful, she now saw, to describe the attachment in ways that made it seem fundamentally unserious and ephemeral.

The whole of Margaret Island was a park, and large enough to forget at times that you were on an island at all. They wandered along its winding asphalt paths. There was an open-air theater and farther on a sort of miniature zoo—delicate-footed deer in a shabby enclosure. Some kids were feeding them through the fence. On all the trees hung limp sprigs of green that would soon be leaves. Spring was unstoppably on its way.

At one point Ursula asked, "You're not pregnant, are you?"

And Miri said, "No."

There was a tension between them. It was difficult to say when exactly it had started but it was there and it was increasingly inhibiting. They were talking less and less.

"Have you told your father?" Ursula asked a few minutes later.

"Not yet," Miri said. "I'm going to London on Wednesday. I'll tell him then. He's got other things to worry about."

"I know. What's the news with that?" Ursula asked.

Miri's father had prostate cancer.

"He's finished the radiotherapy," Miri told her. "That was a few weeks ago. On Thursday he has to go into the hospital to do some scans."

And then Ursula said, "I think I need to sit down for a moment."

"What is it?"

"Nothing. I just feel a bit dizzy."

They sat down on the nearest bench, which was under a tree. In turbulent surges the tree made a hissing sound when the wind went through it.

Ursula felt her blood pressure normalize. She felt securely situated again. Miranda was sitting next to her looking the other way across a wide lawn on which numerous games of football were in progress. She looked so young, Ursula thought. She had one of those stud things in her nose, and the skin around it seemed slightly inflamed. The sight of the inflamed skin made Ursula's eyes fill with tears. She asked herself what it was about the situation—what *exactly* it was—that made her feel so uneasy about it, that made her feel that it was a threat to her daughter's happiness, and therefore to her own. She tried to sort out the things that didn't trouble her from the things that did—they seemed all mixed up together and it was hard to separate them out. *Why do you need to marry him?* she wanted to ask. *Why* marry *him? People don't just automatically do that anymore—why do you need to?* It seemed so absurdly old-fashioned. What was the point?

The extremities of the tree strained in the wind. Ursula sighed.

"Are you all right?" Miri asked.

"Think so." Ursula dabbed her eyes with a paper tissue. "So am I going to see him, Moussa, while I'm here?"

"Of course," Miri said. "He wants to see you."

"When then?"

"Now?" Miri suggested.

"Is he around?"

"Probably." She laughed. "It's not like he has loads to do."

She spoke to him on the phone and then said, "He'll meet us in half an hour."

They walked back through the park to the bridge and took a tram to the place where Moussa had said he would meet them, a Starbucks. "He likes Starbucks," Miri explained.

"Does he?" Ursula asked, unsure what to make of that.

The tram slid along an avenue, making a loud electric hum every time it sped up.

They left it at a noisy intersection and waited at some traffic lights. The Starbucks was on the other side of the road.

He was already there. Ursula spotted him immediately. It was extraordinary, she thought, how differently she saw him now, and in that moment of seeing him, as

he stood up to meet them in the Starbucks, she understood that, in some way, that must have been Miri's purpose in taking the unexpected, the almost melodramatic
step of announcing her intention to marry him: to make
her see him differently.

12

BUD–LGW

She had not seen her father for nearly a year. It had been that long since she was last in London. She felt a tingle of nervousness in her stomach as she emerged from the Tube at Notting Hill Gate. From there it was a short walk to the street where he lived. The layout of the area was familiar to her, and when she turned into the street she saw that the trees that lined it had put out their blossoms—the snow-like excess that lasted for a week or two every spring. She remembered the sight of that, and seeing it she remembered other things as well, like how for years she and her father had walked together every school-day morning to the bus stop on Westbourne Grove. She had spent much of her childhood in this street, had lived here until she was twelve, when her parents separated and her mother took her to live in Germany. Since then, she had only seen her father once or twice a year.

He looked a lot older than the last time she had seen him. It was partly the illness, of course, and the effects of the treatment. He looked shrunken in his open-necked shirt, his hair short, veins forking prominently on his temples. When he embraced her he didn't feel strong. It seemed strange that he was still in his fifties. He was talking about lunch. He seemed to think there was some problem there, though she wasn't sure what it was. "Why don't we just go to the Walmer Castle?" she said.

She went to the loo. The loo, like everything else in the flat, was the same as ever. There was the stack of out-of-date *Time Out*s and music magazines next to the toilet—she had very definite memories of those from her early school days, when they had seemed like mysterious things from an impenetrable adult world. (Their total lack of mystery today was somehow disappointing.) There was the tiny frosted window transmitting the green of the garden, to which the upstairs flat had no other access, and there was the Kennedy quote framed on the wall next to the light switch. *For, in the final analysis, our most basic common link is that we all inhabit this small planet. We all breathe the same air. We all cherish our children's future. And we are all mortal.*

She was in London to be with her father when he went to St. Mary's Hospital for the scans the next day. She had hated the thought of him doing that alone. So that was why she was there. Still, there was the other thing. Her "news"—it would just be weird not to mention that while she was here. When, though? She thought she should probably wait until after the hospital. She didn't want him to feel she was there to talk about herself. And she wasn't sure how he would take her news anyway.

She washed her hands in the tiny sink where the water trickled as feebly from the tap as it always had, and went back to the living room.

"The Walmer Castle?" she suggested again.

Her father seemed even more nervously self-absorbed than normal. "Yeah, okay," he said. He put on old gray Converse trainers and a knee-length navy overcoat and they walked to the pub.

It was while they were there waiting for their pad thais that they first touched on the subject of his illness: she asked him how he was feeling.

He shrugged and said, "Okay."

There was this little unhealed thing between them. When the diagnosis was made, in January, he hadn't told her himself that he had cancer. She had heard it from her grandmother, who lived in Spain. "Why did I have to hear it from her?" she had asked him at the time. He hadn't answered the question then, and they had hardly spoken since. It came up again as they waited for their food. He said, "I was embarrassed. I know that sounds lame."

She had, after some hesitation, ordered a small wine. She took a sip of it.

"I was ashamed," he said. "There's something shameful about it—dying." He laughed. "It's a shit look."

"You're not dying."

"We're all dying, darling."

"You know what I mean."

At that point the food arrived, and anyway there didn't seem to be much more to say on the subject. To talk about anything else, though, seemed impossible as well. So they ended up not talking much at all.

She wondered, as they sat there afterwards while she finished her wine, whether to tell him her news. It didn't feel appropriate somehow, and she let the moment pass, and then he was paying for the meal and they were in the street again.

She suggested that later they might see a film at one of the cinemas at Notting Hill Gate—the Gate, she said, or the Coronet.

"The Coronet's closed," he told her. "Few years ago."

"Oh," she said. "I didn't know." It made her feel like a stranger in the area, not knowing something like that. She said, "Okay. Well why don't we see what's on at the Gate?"

A French film called *Fifty Springtimes* was on that evening. Neither of them had heard of it and they stood outside wondering whether to get tickets. She read out

the film's description in the program: *"César Award win-
ner Agnès Jaoui gives an intelligent and affecting perfor-
mance as Aurore; fifty, flirty, and not-so-thriving, her world
is turned upside down when a past flame returns, reignit-
ing her lust for life and love. A witty and wonderful ode to
embracing age whilst staying young."*

"Oh for fuck's sake," her father said.

"Doesn't that sound okay?"

"Embracing age whilst staying young? What does that
even mean? And who says *whilst* anymore anyway? It's
absurd."

"I think we should see it," she said. She thought it
might be preferable for them not to spend the whole evening in the flat.

Her father insisted on paying for the tickets.

That afternoon he had a lie-down, which he never
used to do. She spoke to Moussa on Viber, almost whis-
pering in the living room, as if she was a teenager, and
then, as her father was still asleep, she went for a soli-
tary walk around the area. She eyed Westbourne Grove
with a kind of distaste—used to the streets of a much
poorer city now, she was slightly shocked by its parade of
wealth. She felt what seemed like the fundamental hostil-
ity of the place—with its evident obsession with money
and status—to someone like Moussa, who was entirely
without either.

She had a half-pint on her own in the Sun in Splendour, wondering what she was doing in London. Her father didn't seem particularly pleased that she was there, and the place itself seemed foreign to her. She missed Moussa. She walked back to the flat and made a light supper out of some things she had picked up from Sainsbury's, which she and her father ate together, though neither of them had much of an appetite. As they ate, he asked her about her work at CEU, and she told him something about it. Though he made an effort to seem interested, she felt very aware, as she always did with him, of her own seriousness, a quality that never seemed to fit properly with his kind of Englishness—ironic, mocking, and evasive.

He asked her when she was going to get her doctorate.

"About two years," she told him.

"I hope I live that long," he said, and laughed.

After supper they went to see the film.

She didn't sleep well. She was on the sofa, which unfolded into a flimsy bed. It was odd and unsettling to lie there surrounded by the looming shapes of the living room. It wasn't properly dark—a streetlight outside the window shone in through the pale blind. She was troubled by a sense of separation from her own past. She was also troubled, in another way, by the fact that she hadn't yet told her father her news. There in the semidarkness, it seemed starkly obvious to her that she had to tell him before they went to the hospital in the morning, that if she waited until afterwards, it might be too late.

"I have something to tell you," she said. "Moussa and I are getting married."

He stared at her for a moment, and then asked, quite pleasantly, "He's not some nutcase is he?"

She stared at him, wondering what to make of the question. Finally she said, "No, I don't think he's a nutcase."

"You know," her father said, and he was still smiling, "some Islamic nutter?"

"He's not like that."

"Moussa?" He lifted his mug to his mouth. It was the next morning. They were sitting at the kitchen table. Neither of them was eating anything.

"That's his name, yes."

"Moses."

"Yes."

"Do you love him?" he asked.

"Yes," she said, feeling that she mustn't hesitate or seem even slightly unsure.

"Well that's the important thing, I suppose. Why doesn't he come and visit?"

"Why doesn't he come to London?"

"Yes."

She said, "He has an expired Syrian passport—might be a problem at Heathrow?"

Her father laughed at that. He seemed very amused by the whole situation. "Yes, it might."

"He's not allowed to leave Hungary," she explained.

"No?"

"It's where he was granted asylum."

"I thought the nasty Hungarians didn't do that sort of thing."

"They used to. He arrived in early 2015."

"Ah. Well," her father said, "maybe I'll come and meet him there. If I live long enough that is. . . ."

"Will you stop saying things like that," she said.

Her tone took him by surprise.

"Please," she said, "just stop saying things like that. I know you find it hard to be serious about anything."

She had never spoken to him in that way before. She had no idea how he would take it. She waited, looking at him, feeling unexpectedly euphoric.

"I'm sorry," he said. "I'm frightened."

"I know, I understand. . . ."

"That's why I say things like that."

"I know," she said. "But some things *are* serious. Which *is* frightening."

Though she didn't want it, she poured the last of the coffee from the cafetière into her mug. He had had that cafetière for as long as she could remember, all her life. Neither of them seemed to know what to say next. She looked at her watch. "We should go soon," she said. His appointment at the hospital was in an hour.

They put on their shoes and jackets and were about to leave when he stopped for a moment at the door and said, "I'm happy you're here."

"That's okay," she said.

They went down the stairs. It was still quite early, a few minutes after eight. They walked to the bus stop on Westbourne Grove. Clouds moved in the sky, the sun came and went, and as they reached the corner the wind dislodged blossoms from all the trees in the street.

ABOUT THE AUTHOR

David Szalay was born in Canada and moved to London as a small child. He has published five novels, including *London and the South-East*, which won the Betty Trask Prize and the Geoffrey Faber Memorial Prize, and *All That Man Is*, which was shortlisted for the 2016 Man Booker Prize and won the 2016 Gordon Burn Prize; it has been translated into nearly twenty languages. He lives in Budapest.

LES AVENTURES EXTRAORDINAIRES DE

HERCULE

D0888181

Claudia Zeff
Adaptation de Gill Harvey

Illustrations de
Stephen Cartwright

Texte français de France Gladu

Éditions
SCHOLASTIC

Table des matières

Chapitre 1

La déesse jalouse

Il y a très longtemps, de l'union du grand dieu Zeus et d'une humaine est né un fils prénommé Hercule. Tous les dieux adorent l'enfant… Tous?

Enfin presque, car la déesse Héra en est tout de suite jalouse…

3

« Je vais me débarrasser de lui », se dit Héra. Elle lâche des serpents venimeux dans le berceau d'Hercule.

Sssssssss... aaaaaaaaah!

Mais Hercule est déjà si fort qu'il étrangle sans peine les serpents. Héra est furieuse.

Plus Hercule grandit, plus il devient fort. Un jour, il apprend qu'un méchant seigneur a volé les vaches du roi de Thèbes.

Hercule provoque le seigneur en duel. Puis il attend, seul sur un petit sentier, et tue un à un les soldats du seigneur.

Le roi de Thèbes est enchanté.
— Merci! s'écrie-t-il. Tu peux épouser
ma fille Mégère en récompense.

Hercule et Mégère sont très heureux et
ont trois beaux garçons. Hercule adore
leur enseigner tout ce qu'il sait.

Mais la jalousie d'Héra ne cesse de grandir.

Je vais lui jeter un mauvais sort!

Ensorcelé par Héra, Hercule devient soudain fou et tue ses fils bien-aimés. Puis il est rongé par le chagrin.
— Qu'est-ce que j'ai fait! se lamente-t-il.

Il se précipite au temple pour demander pardon. Une prêtresse écoute sa prière.

— Va voir le roi Eurysthée, déclare-t-elle. Il te donnera douze tâches.

Tu trouveras le roi Eurysthée à Tirynthe.

Si tu les exécutes toutes, les dieux te pardonneront.

Chapitre 2

Les tâches

Hercule va trouver le roi.
— Quelles sont mes tâches? demande-
t-il.
— Un énorme lion rôde dans les
parages, dit le roi.

Ta première
tâche est
de le tuer!

Hercule pourchasse le lion durant un mois. Enfin, il l'aperçoit près d'une caverne. Il s'élance et tente de le tuer d'un coup d'épée...

... mais le lion a la peau trop dure. Hercule l'assomme alors d'un coup de massue. Le lion est surpris, mais il vit encore.

Hercule se glisse derrière l'énorme animal et le suit dans la caverne. Soudain, le lion bondit sur lui.

Ils roulent sur le sol et luttent pendant des heures. Enfin, Hercule saisit le fauve à la gorge et l'étrangle.

En voyant le lion, le roi est terrifié.

— Il n'y a rien à craindre, dit Hercule.
Il est mort.

Mais le roi est si effrayé qu'il saute
dans un grand vase de laiton.

— Va tuer l'Hydre! crie-t-il. C'est ta
prochaine tâche.

L'Hydre est un horrible monstre à neuf têtes qui vit dans un lugubre marais. Accompagné de son neveu, Hercule s'apprête à partir. C'est alors que paraît la déesse Athéna.

Il faut lancer des flèches de feu pour faire sortir l'Hydre.

— Une seule bouffée de son poison vous tuera, les prévient-elle. Alors, retenez votre souffle.

13

Hercule s'approche de la tanière de l'Hydre. Il noue des poignées d'herbe à ses flèches, les allume, puis les lance dans la tanière.

Il entend un effroyable sifflement. L'Hydre sort de son repaire! Ses neuf têtes apparaissent et crachent du poison.

Hercule retient son souffle et fonce sur le monstre.

D'un coup puissant, il fait
tomber l'une
des têtes les
plus affreuses.
La tête lance
un hurlement
horrible, puis
s'écrase au sol.

Mais deux
autres têtes
poussent
aussitôt à
sa place!

Quoi?!

16

Hercule réagit rapidement. Il enflamme sa lance et fonce de nouveau sur l'Hydre.

Dès qu'il a fini de couper une tête, il brûle aussitôt le cou pour empêcher qu'une autre pousse. C'est ainsi qu'il réussit finalement à tuer l'Hydre.

Chapitre 3

Un cerf et un sanglier

La troisième tâche d'Hercule consiste à attraper un cerf aux cornes d'or. Il pourchasse l'animal durant toute une année, mais sans succès.

Puis un jour, près d'une rivière,
Hercule voit quelque chose briller au
soleil. « Les cornes d'or », se dit-il.

Sur la pointe des pieds, Hercule se rend à la rivière avec son filet. Occupé à boire paisiblement, le cerf ne l'entend pas venir.

Soudain, Hercule s'élance et jette son filet sur l'animal. Le voilà pris au piège!

Le cerf lutte et se débat jusqu'à
épuisement. Lorsqu'il est enfin
immobile, Hercule attache ensemble
ses sabots d'or. Puis il hisse le cerf sur
ses épaules.
— En route! dit-il.

Mais en traversant péniblement la
forêt, Hercule voit une femme qui
s'avance vers lui.

— Arrête! ordonne-t-elle. Je suis la déesse Artémis et ceci est mon cerf.

Tu peux le montrer au roi, mais tu dois promettre de ne lui faire aucun mal.
— J'en prendrai grand soin, dit Hercule, et il continue sa route.

— Bien joué, Hercule! dit le roi.
Maintenant, attrape un sanglier.

Hercule se rend chez son ami le
centaure. Mi-homme, mi-cheval,
il sait où vit chaque animal.
— Salut, Hercule!
lance-t-il. Prends le
chemin des
montagnes. Mais
avant, buvons un
coup ensemble!

Un peu plus tard, Hercule prend
la route des montagnes. Il
marche très longtemps et
met des heures à repérer
le sanglier.
Enfin, il le voit, perché
tout en haut d'une
montagne.

Mais le sanglier
est énorme
et féroce.
Comment faire
pour l'attraper?

24

« Je vais devoir faire preuve d'astuce »,
se dit Hercule. Lentement, il traque
le sanglier… plus haut, toujours plus
haut dans les montagnes.

Parfait…
je vais finir par
t'avoir!

Lorsqu'il atteint la neige, au sommet,
le sanglier est si gros et si malhabile
qu'il tombe dans un banc de neige.
— Je t'ai eu! s'écrie Hercule.

Il s'empresse d'enchaîner la bête. Son butin sur le dos, il retourne à grand-peine chez le roi.

En voyant le sanglier, le roi saute de nouveau dans son vase.
— Ta prochaine tâche consiste à nettoyer les écuries du roi Augias… en un jour! déclare-t-il.

26

Chapitre 4

Des rivières
et des oiseaux

Le roi Augias éclate d'un grand rire en
entendant la tâche confiée à Hercule.
— Viens voir mes écuries, s'esclaffe-
t-il. Personne ne les a nettoyées depuis
trente ans!

Une journée?
Impossible!

Le roi Augias a raison. Les écuries sont sales et malodorantes. Hercule regarde autour de lui et réfléchit. Puis il sourit. « Ça ne devrait pas être bien difficile », songe-t-il.

Tôt le lendemain, il se met à l'œuvre. À coups de massue, il perce un grand trou à chaque extrémité des écuries.

Puis, il gravit une colline à proximité où deux rivières se rencontrent et coulent dans une vallée. Hercule dresse alors un barrage avec d'énormes pierres.

Il travaille toute la journée, sous un soleil de plomb. Le soir venu, les rivières détournées coulent vers les écuries.

L'eau traverse à vive allure les écuries, emportant toute la saleté. En quelques minutes, l'endroit reluit.

Peu avant le coucher du soleil, Hercule défait le barrage et répare les murs des écuries. Voilà la cinquième tâche accomplie.

30

Hercule reçoit pour sixième tâche de tuer une volée d'affreux oiseaux. Ceux-ci déchirent les animaux, en font leur festin et dévorent même les humains. Hercule se met en route.

Les oiseaux vivent sur une île au milieu d'un marais. Hercule essaie de ramer vers l'île, mais le marais est trop boueux. Sa chaloupe reste coincée.

Comment atteindre les oiseaux?

« La déesse Athéna m'aidera peut-être »,
songe-t-il. Et en un éclair, elle apparaît!

— Prends ce hochet d'or, dit-elle. Si tu
l'agites, les oiseaux auront peur et
s'envoleront.

Quand
ils prendront leur
envol, tu les
abattras!

Le bruit du hochet rend Hercule
presque sourd. Mais l'idée était bonne.
Effrayés, les oiseaux tournoient dans
le ciel en poussant des cris perçants.

Depuis la terre ferme, Hercule leur
décoche des flèches. Il rapporte sa plus
grosse prise au roi.

Chapitre 5

Des taureaux et des chevaux

Une fois mort, l'oiseau ne semble pas si dangereux.

— Ha! Ce n'est qu'un petit oiseau, dit le roi. Va plutôt capturer le grand taureau blanc, en Crète!

La Crête est une île lointaine. Hercule trouve donc un navire pour s'y rendre. Le roi Minos, qui règne sur l'île, l'accueille et le conduit à son magnifique palais.

> Je suis venu chercher le grand taureau.

> Ah, parfait! Emmène-le loin d'ici!

— Ce taureau est une calamité, dit le roi Minos. Il tue les gens et fait des ravages sur l'île.

Hercule trouve le taureau dans une oliveraie. Il piaffe de ses monstrueux sabots et ses naseaux soufflent des gerbes de feu.

Hercule tente de le surprendre, mais le taureau l'aperçoit et charge.

Heureusement, Hercule porte la peau du lion qu'il a tué. Celle-ci le protège du souffle brûlant de la bête.

Il saisit les cornes redoutables du
taureau. L'animal lutte sauvagement,
mais Hercule tient bon. Enfin, l'animal
s'effondre, épuisé.

Lorsque le roi aperçoit le taureau, il est terrorisé.

— Rapporte-moi les chevaux du roi Diomède! glapit-il. Ils mangent les gens!

> Hercule?
> Je suis Diomède.
> Entre, mon brave...

Hercule se rend donc au château de Diomède avec quatre de ses amis. Diomède paraît amical, mais Hercule s'en méfie.

— Je crois que Diomède projette de nous tuer, dit-il à ses amis. Il faudra prendre les chevaux dès ce soir.
À la nuit tombée, ils se faufilent jusqu'aux écuries.

Hercule démolit les portes. Les chevaux sauvages sont enchaînés à une poutre. Il coupe leurs chaînes d'un coup de hache.

Hercule et ses amis se précipitent vers leur navire avec les chevaux. Mais avant qu'ils aient pu fuir, le roi Diomède apprend ce qu'ils ont fait. Avec des soldats, il se lance à la poursuite d'Hercule.

Mais Diomède ne fait pas le poids
contre Hercule et ses amis.
Bientôt, tous les soldats
sont morts. Hercule tue
lui-même Diomède et
le donne en pâture
aux chevaux.

Après l'avoir dévoré, les chevaux
deviennent dociles.
— À présent, retournons voir ce roi
ridicule dans son vase! dit Hercule.

Chapitre 6

Des amazones et des ogres

La neuvième tâche d'Hercule consiste à rapporter la ceinture d'Hippolyte, reine des Amazones. Les Amazones sont des guerrières acharnées que personne n'a jamais vues.
Avec un navire rempli d'hommes, Hercule part à leur recherche.

À sa grande surprise, Hippolyte est gentille.

— Je suis venu chercher ta ceinture, lui dit Hercule.

— Tu n'auras pas à combattre pour l'obtenir, dit-elle en souriant.

Je t'en fais cadeau.

Tu en es sûre?

Elle offre un merveilleux festin à Hercule et à tout son équipage.

43

Mais la déesse Héra est toujours jalouse d'Hercule. Elle déteste le voir s'amuser.

Elle se déguise donc en amazone et se mêle à la fête.

— Hercule est ici pour assassiner notre reine, chuchote-t-elle aux femmes.

Méfiez-vous de lui!

Les Amazones se lèvent d'un bond.
Elles attaquent Hercule et ses hommes
avec leurs épées.

Durant le combat, Hercule tue
Hippolyte. Il saisit sa ceinture et
s'enfuit.

— Tous au bateau! hurle-t-il à ses
hommes.

Mais les Amazones les pourchassent.
Une terrible bataille s'engage.

Durant des heures, les Amazones
semblent sur le point de
l'emporter. Mais Hercule
et ses hommes résistent.

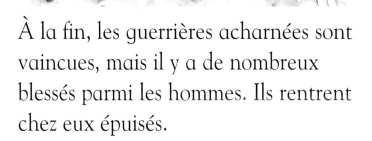

À la fin, les guerrières acharnées sont
vaincues, mais il y a de nombreux
blessés parmi les hommes. Ils rentrent
chez eux épuisés.

Les hommes peuvent se reposer,
mais Hercule a encore
trois tâches à exécuter.
— Trouve Géryon,
l'ogre à trois têtes,
et rapporte-moi ses
vaches, dit le roi.

Géryon vit sur une île près de l'Afrique.
Un autre long et épuisant voyage
s'annonce.
Hélios, le dieu du soleil, a pitié

d'Hercule. Il
lui envoie un
lotus en guise
de bateau pour
s'y rendre.

Hercule explore l'île de Géryon et ne tarde pas à trouver l'ogre et ses vaches. Mais avant qu'il puisse s'approcher d'eux, un chien féroce à deux têtes se jette sur lui.

Hercule frappe le chien de son gourdin et tue ainsi l'animal sur-le-champ.

49

Hercule se dirige vers les vaches.
L'ogre se tient debout au milieu de leur pâturage.
Dissimulé derrière un rocher, Hercule pose sur son arc une flèche empoisonnée.

Il est énorme!

Il est difficile d'atteindre l'ogre sous cet angle.

— Géryon! crie Hercule.

L'ogre se retourne. Hercule tire bien vite une flèche qui transperce les trois corps.

Géryon s'effondre, mort sur le coup. Hercule rassemble les vaches sur son bateau-lotus et file chez le roi.

Plus que deux tâches

— Tu en as mis du temps, grogne le roi. Maintenant, trouve l'arbre des Hespérides. Je veux trois de ses pommes d'or.

L'arbre se trouve à l'autre bout de la Terre où Atlas, un imposant géant, soutient le ciel.

— Comment puis-je prendre ces pommes? demande Hercule à Atlas.

— Tu dois d'abord tuer le dragon qui garde l'arbre, lui répond-il. Mais je suis le seul à pouvoir cueillir les pommes.

Hercule repère le dragon, lui envoie une flèche mortelle et revient voir Atlas.

53

— Si tu veux bien tenir le ciel à ma place, j'irai cueillir les pommes, dit le géant.
Hercule attend… et attend… et attend…

Atlas prend tout son temps pour cueillir les pommes. Il n'est pas pressé de retourner soutenir le ciel.

Je vais lui proposer d'aller moi-même porter les pommes au roi!

Mais Hercule est plus futé qu'Atlas.
— Avant de te rendre chez le roi,
pourrais-tu me montrer encore comment
je dois tenir le ciel? lui demande-t-il.

Il a fallu dix ans à Hercule pour exécuter les onze premières tâches. Il est exténué, mais il ne lui en reste plus qu'une.

— Va chercher Cerbère, dit le roi.

— Mais c'est le chien qui garde les enfers! s'exclame Hercule.

La tâche semble impossible, mais le dieu Hermès et la déesse Athéna proposent de le guider.

Après un long et sombre voyage, ils atteignent la rivière Styx. Il faut la traverser pour se rendre aux enfers, mais Charon, le vieux passeur, refuse de les emmener.

Finalement, Charon accepte d'emmener Hercule, mais ne laisse embarquer ni Hermès, ni Athéna.

Hercule atteint l'autre rive sain et sauf et erre parmi les fantômes qui murmurent de leur étrange voix éteinte.

Il traverse le pays des morts et arrive chez le roi et la reine. Il s'agenouille devant eux et leur demande le chien.

— J'en prendrai soin, promet Hercule, qui regagne la rivière Styx pour retrouver le chien.

Cerbère garde la
porte des enfers.
Chacune de
ses trois têtes
est couronnée
d'une crinière
de serpents
qui sifflent et
se tortillent.
Il est vraiment
terrifiant.

Alors qu'Hercule
s'approche, Cerbère
bondit. Hercule
s'élance et
attrape le
chien.

Après une longue lutte, le chien s'écrase au sol, vaincu. Hercule le ramène de l'autre côté de la rivière Styx, puis chez le roi Eurysthée.

Voici Cerbère. J'ai exécuté mes douze tâches!

Comme toujours, le roi ne semble pas enchanté de revoir Hercule.

Hercule va droit au temple voir la prêtresse.

— Les dieux t'ont pardonné d'avoir tué tes fils, dit-elle.

Les autres dieux sont fiers d'Hercule. Ils l'accueillent chez eux, sur le mont Olympe, et veillent sur lui depuis ce jour.

Dans cette collection

NIVEAU 4

Les aventures
extraordinaires
d'Hercule

Dracula

Le fantôme
du parc

L'incroyable
cadeau

On a d'abord raconté l'histoire d'Hercule il y a quelque
3 000 ans dans la Grèce antique. Hercule était le héros grec
le plus fort, mais les Grecs l'appelaient Héraclès. Nous avons
utilisé son nom romain qui est Hercule parce que ce héros
est beaucoup mieux connu sous ce nom aujourd'hui.

Conception graphique : Katarina Dragoslavić

Catalogage avant publication de Bibliothèque et Archives Canada

Zeff, Claudia

Les aventures extraordinaires de Hercule / renarré par Claudia Zeff ;
illustrations, Stephen Cartwright ; texte français de France Gladu.

(Petit poisson deviendra grand)
Traduction de: The amazing adventures of Hercules.
Pour les 7 ans et plus.
ISBN 978-0-545-98295-5

I. Cartwright, Stephen, 1947- II. Gladu, France, 1957- III. Titre.
IV. Collection: Petit poisson deviendra grand (Toronto, Ont.)

PZ24.1.Z44Av 2010   j823'.914   C2009-904444-7

Édition publiée par les Éditions Scholastic,
604, rue King Ouest, Toronto (Ontario) M5V 1E1,
avec la permission d'Usborne Publishing Ltd.

5 4 3 2 1   Imprimé à Singapour 46   09 10 11 12 13